# Stories from the Attic

*by Marcina McKeon Foster*

This story is inspired by real people and events. My intent is to bring our many family stories to life and to introduce our descendants to their ancestors. Family members in this story are all real people. However, this book is a work of fiction. Although most events were inspired by letters, diaries and family lore; the dramatization is fictitious. Other events and some minor characters are entirely my imagination. I have made my best effort to portray facts and events accurately.

# Stories

FROM
THE

## Attic

*Stories From the Attic*
*by Marcina McKeon Foster*
*Copyright ©2020 Marcina McKeon Foster*

*1st Printing 2020*
*ISBN: 978-1-7351012-1-7 (paperback)*
*ISBN: 978-1-7351012-0-0 (hardcover)*
*Library of Congress Control Number: 2020911067*

*Marcina L Foster*
*510 Veranda Way Suite 101*
*Naples Fl 34104*
*Marcie.foster@hotmail.com*
*Stories from the Attic*

*Cover design and layout by Canoe Circle Graphics*
*Editing by Terie Spencer*
*Cover art by William Brody (www.wbrody.com)*

*Printed in the U.S.A.*

# Dedication

This book is dedicated to my sister, Jean McKeon Martin, who has taken this journey with me into our family's past, from the discovery of the letters written by our great-grandfather's half-sister Bessie Shields to our treks up and down the streets of Fenton, Michigan. She has been my research partner and friend, finding obscure bits of information, wracking our brains together to figure out who, what, when, where, why and how. It's been fun!

# Table of Contents

# PART 1

## Lake Fenton

# 1
## *The Cottage*

Scott Cottage—Lake Fenton

The old saying, "If these walls could talk" resonates with me as I study my family's past. In addition to people, the significance of buildings looms large in our history. They are not just brick and mortar—they hold memories and mysteries of the past.

One especially stands out in my mind: the family cottage we traveled to each year. The summer of 1962, when I was ten years old, was the last season we spent there. That June, as always, the cottage came to life upon our arrival and hummed with activity all summer long. My family made memories there that have lasted for decades.

The cottage also had its own memories, waiting to be discovered by younger generations. Through old photographs, odd objects and mysterious rooms, our summer home provided an intriguing glimpse into history. Year after year, my fascination with its past never lessened.

Getting ready for summer at the Lake Fenton cottage was a whirlwind of activity for the whole family. Mom got out our summer clothes, handing down shorts and tops I'd outgrown to my younger sisters. She packed groceries, snacks, drinks and even food for Mitzi, the cat. Dad got the station wagon ready. He checked the oil, the air pressure in the tires, and the water in the battery.

My brother, sisters and I had to pack our books and toys and choose our tennis shoes. This was an important decision because we only got two pairs of shoes each year: school shoes in September—the dreaded saddle shoes—and tennis shoes in the summer—PF Flyers.

PF Flyers came in three colors: white, red and blue. No self-respecting child ever chose white. I usually picked blue, my favorite color. Size was an issue, too. Mom always made us get a half size too big so we could "grow into them."

I loved going to Lake Fenton and couldn't wait for our vacation to start. As soon as school was out, our big noisy family piled into the "woody" station wagon and headed to the cottage. I couldn't imagine spending the summer anywhere else. Dad spent the summer commuting by train to his job at Ford Tractor Company in Birmingham. He left every Monday and returned Friday nights. We kids and mom got to spend the entire summer at the lake!

There is a pecking order in a large family, based on age. Since I was the oldest, I was the least aware of the unspoken rules of car rides. They were always followed exactly, however, and this is what the pecking order looked like inside the station wagon:

Dad drove. Mom sat in the front with him. The baby, Karen, sat between them in a turquoise-colored vinyl car seat hooked over the bench seat. She played with a toy steering wheel as the rest of us kids scrambled into our seats.

I sat behind Mom. My brother Jimmy, a year younger than me, sat behind Dad. Our middle sister Jean sat in the middle on the "hump" or rode in the way-back on a blanket with Becky. The annoying seatbelts were tucked under the cushions, out of the way, and the car windows were down.

We loved watching the landmarks as Dad navigated the two-hour drive. The ski resort billboard proclaiming *Our Business is Going Downhill* was a favorite, as was the travel trailer perched high on a post to advertise a recreational vehicle dealership. After the big purple barn on the corner, the road became dirt. We passed rows of narrow frame cottages baking in the sun until the woods— shady, cool and quiet—came into view. A wooden wagon wheel holding three mailboxes mounted on a post stood sentry, signaling that we were getting closer.

As we drove onto Crane's Pointe, the road narrowed to two worn tire tracks. Excitement grew as we glimpsed the lake on both sides of the road. There were only three houses on Crane's Pointe. First was the large stone house and white barn belonging to Celia Crane. Celia's horse, named "Glory Be," roamed the property freely, nibbling on grass and sticking his head in any open window.

The second house was our grandparents' cottage, a white two-story Georgian. I thought this house was beautiful with its dormers, green shutters, and a large screened-in side porch. Our grandparents were our Mom's parents, Nellie Phillips Scott and William Colwell Scott, or Nonie and Gramp as we called them.

At the end of Crane's Pointe was the third house, a worn, ramshackle two-story frame building with a stone fireplace on the side porch. This had been Edith Crane's home during the last years of her life. The story about how our grandparents' cottage originated was rather bizarre. In the 1920s and 1930s Celia and Edith Crane operated a girls' camp on Crane's Pointe. There was a large lodge that was the dormitory, social hall, dining room and kitchen of Crane's Pointe Camp. During World War II, the camp closed. The Crane sisters decided to sell half of the lodge to my grandparents and Edith would live in the other half. But it was not to be a duplex-type arrangement. They decided to physically divide the lodge.

According to Mom, Gramp and my two uncles actually sawed the big building in half. They rolled their half across the lot on logs, then built a new wall to close up the house. When Mom told the story, she explained that materials were scarce during the war. Gramp and his sons used whatever was available, even straightening old nails to be reused. Under those circumstances, I guess dividing the house made more sense than building a new one. Even so, I had a hard time believing the story, except when I was confronted with that huge stone fireplace sitting on the porch of Miss Crane's half of the lodge. That was proof.

Dad pulled up to the cottage and parked. We had arrived. Bursting out of the car, we raced upstairs to claim our sleeping spaces. There were two large bedrooms on each end of the house and a smaller bedroom in the middle. Mom and Dad got the first large bedroom, at the top of the stairs, next to the bathroom.

Bill Scott, Phil Scott, John Scott and Wally Swanson rebuilding the cottage

My brother and three younger sisters shared the far bedroom. This room was large, but furnished haphazardly. One double bed sat on exposed metal springs and another double bed mattress just lay on the floor. An old crib stood in a corner.

I got the small middle bedroom all to myself. Years before when my mother was a girl this had been her bedroom at the cottage. I tried to imagine Mom in that very room, years ago. Had she sat on this same double bed, talking to her best friend, Barb? Had she sat at this same dressing table, fixing her hair? There was a funny little chair next to the table. My mother called it a cricket chair. Had she sat there reading, as I loved to do? One of the windows was small and turned on end to make it diamond-shaped. Had that been her idea when they fixed up the cottage?

Three formal wedding pictures hung on the wall, one for my parents and one for each of my aunts and uncles. I spent hours marveling at them when they were young. The different styles of clothing fascinated me. My mom's dress was long draping satin, her train elegantly pooling on the floor. My Aunt Bev's was also traditional—floor-length lace and taffeta—but Aunt Sandy's dress was cocktail length and full-skirted. Sandy looked so cute and modern with her short blond bob and veil. I would lay there in bed, looking at the pictures and imagining the weddings. Eventually, I fell asleep to the drone of motor boats out on the lake.

The first morning of vacation always seemed to be bright and beautiful. On the lake, sunlight sparkled like diamonds on the water. The distant hum of motor boats signaled the start of summer. The dock sat stacked in sections on the shore, waiting to be put in. The lake bottom was mucky, since Dad had yet to rake the sand to make a clean swimming area.

Left to right: John & Bev Scott, Jim & Shirley McKeon with Marcie McKeon, Bill & Nellie Scott, Clifford Phillips, Sandy and Phil Scott

The whole summer stretched out before us. Warm, sunny days would be filled with swimming, climbing trees, catching tadpoles, and digging in the clay dirt. The cool nights were for catching fireflies, roasting marshmallows, and listening to the grownups talk.

Down by the water's edge, two ancient wooden rowboats sat upside down on sawhorses. They belonged to my uncles years ago and appeared quite unseaworthy. But in the summer of 1962, Dad launched one. It floated! We kids spent many hours rowing my mother around the cove. I'm sure she was glad we had an activity that used up so much youthful energy.

Dad's fourteen-foot speedboat with a big Evinrude & Johnson outboard motor was moored along the side of the white wooden dock. When not in use, it was covered with a canvas tarp. That was my favorite spot to sunbathe—lying on the hot tarp, the boat bobbing gently on the water.

There was an island on the lake which you could see from our cottage. Mom's best friend from high school, Barb Asbury, had a cottage there. The island was so close we could have swum across if we weren't afraid of being hit by a speedboat or getting covered with muck in that shallow, muddy area. So instead of swimming, we rowed our little boat across. Many fun-filled days were spent on the island, playing and exploring. At the far end was a park with a picnic area and a huge wooden platform swing and a well hand pump. A dozen children could sit on that platform and slowly swing back and forth. It was mesmerizing.

While we kids reacquainted ourselves with the outdoors at our summer cottage, Mom worked inside, cleaning the dust and spider webs which had built up over the winter. Once tidied up, the cottage was comfortable and charming. The ceilings were held up with rustic, rough-sawn beams. The furnishings were a jumbled, eclectic mix of antique couches, chairs and tables. My grandmother, Nonie, had quirkily painted the individual bricks on the fireplace pink, green and yellow.

I was fascinated by the old free-standing RCA Victrola in the living room. In the cabinet was a collection of vintage 75-rpm records from the World War I era. My favorite was "Over There." It stirred my imagination to operate the machine with the hand crank and listen to the lively song. Images formed in my mind of Yanks in their doughboy uniforms sailing across the Atlantic to fight in a war many years before my time.

On the other side of the foyer was a recreation room, filled with an array of castoffs. Among them were a ping pong table with no net, an old upright piano out of tune and missing keys, a grey upholstered bench seat taken out of an old car, and a china cabinet with three lone bisque doll heads. Tucked behind this room were a bathroom and a bedroom that were only used if Nonie and Gramp came to stay.

There were many more treasures throughout the cottage just waiting to be discovered by inquisitive children. They included Uncle Phil's collection of foreign coins brought back from his wartime service in Germany, a very large seashell ashtray inlaid with mother-of-pearl, a collection of small toys including an old Gumby and Pokey, a gyro wheel and a Newton's cradle, which was a toy with five clicking metal balls suspended from strings. Upstairs, the storage area under the eaves also held a variety of interesting objects: a pink flapper dress, high shoes that buttoned up, a wooden folding wash stand, and lawyers' bookcases. It was a perfect place to explore on a rainy day. Even when the weather didn't cooperate, summer at the cottage was never boring.

Mom reasoned that since we were swimming in the lake all day, there was no need for baths except on Saturday nights. We agreed. All cleaned up for Sunday morning, the family attended Mass at St. John's Catholic Church in Fenton. My father had grown up on a farm on Ray Road just outside Fenton. His father and grandfather had helped build St. John's. Dad's parents, Grandma and Grandpa McKeon, still lived on the Ray Road farm. We visited them often. So when we weren't at the cottage, we were on the farm—watching baby chicks, bringing the cows in from pasture, climbing apple trees, playing in the hayloft or helping Grandma snap beans. It was pretty perfect.

Occasionally we would go into the village of Fenton to visit our great-grandfather on my mother's side, Clifford Phillips. He and his second wife lived in a grand white house with a big stone foundation that sat on the corner of Main Street and Thurber. This splendid Queen Anne was quite a contrast to the contemporary three-bedroom ranch where we lived in Oak Park. The front corner of Granddad's house had been cut at an angle, and above it was a small arched window. Stone steps led up to the covered porch. To the right of the porch was the front door. On the other side of the house was another porch, screened and covered in heavy vines. Mom called it a "sleeping porch." Back behind the house was a tiny wooden detached garage that had been converted into an apartment. It looked like an oversized playhouse to us children. Out in front, a wooden sign was painted with the word "Roomers." When I was old enough to read, I asked about the sign and was told my great-grandparents rented rooms to working men. I accepted that explanation even though I didn't really understand it.

Inside the house to the left was the living room. During our visits, we sat on the horsehair sofa under the half-moon window, with our mother in the middle. Granddad sat in his easy chair. Grandma Fran sat in a straight-backed chair, her legs folded at the ankle and tucked, very lady-like.

We knew that Grandma Fran was not our "real" great-grandmother. Granddad's first wife, Mabel, had died before I was born. Nonie and Gramp talked about "Mother Mabel" all the time. From the wonderful stories I heard,

I wished I could have known her.

Conversations with the elderly relatives were mundane: "My, how you've grown! How do you like school?" Sitting on the itchy horsehair for what seemed like hours, we were as polite as could be, although a little restless.

We were rarely allowed into the other rooms in Granddad's house. The dining room was visible from our perch on the sofa. Beyond the dining room was the door to the kitchen. I only saw the kitchen once. I wish I remembered it.

I do remember the cellar, however. It was damp, dark and scary. For some reason, the large cistern that held rain water was one of the creepiest things I ever encountered. I still shiver when I think about it.

To the right of the living room was my great-grandparents' bedroom and bathroom. Occasionally, Grandma Fran would take us into the bathroom to see the old-fashioned bathtub. She had painted its claw feet with red fingernail polish. That was a memorable sight.

For many years, I thought my great-grandfather was an invalid, because he never moved out of his easy chair during our visits. I figured he could barely walk. However, when it was time for us to leave, he stood up and slowly walked us to the door, proving that he was not confined to his chair after all.

A large skeleton key hung next to the front door. As part of our goodbye ritual, we always asked him about it—and we always got the same reply. He would take the key down from its hook and tell us it was from the Tower of London in England. We clamored for an explanation: did he steal it? Was he in jail in England? Granddad would just chuckle. As Nonie often said, "That's to make little girls ask questions."

# 2

## *Discoveries*

Those summer memories always stayed with me. More family memories and history surfaced years later, when Dad moved to assisted living and we faced the monumental task of cleaning out his house. He and Mom had grown up during the Great Depression, and they saved everything.

Going through old boxes and bags, I recalled that Christmas and birthday presents were unwrapped slowly—slicing the tape with the jackknife Dad always carried, then carefully folding the wrapping paper to be reused. Boxes and ribbons were also saved. "Don't believe the box!" we would shout when someone unwrapped a gift in a box marked "Hudson's" or "Winkleman's." It was a friendly warning that the gift inside was most likely handmade and not store bought.

You can imagine the glut of items stored in our parents' basement over the years. After helping him move to assisted living, much of the stuff ended up in my basement. I kept the leather-bound albums filled with black and white photos of antique cars and ladies in long dresses and wide-brimmed hats. Two large boxes were full of genealogical research compiled by someone called "Cousin Walter." In addition, boxes and crates of cards, letters, photos and other memorabilia found their way to my home. The prospect of going through it all was daunting.

I started sorting the photographs, organizing them chronologically and then by family. I began one album for my mother's family and one for my father's family. As I worked on the memorabilia, photos kept turning up in the most unexpected places. One would be stuck in a folder, others among letters. Just when I thought I was finished, more would turn up in another unexpected place. There was no rhyme or reason to it. The pile of photos on my pool table grew and grew. I bought more albums, more photo protectors. Most of the snapshots were not labeled. I drafted my sister Jean's assistance in identification and was grateful for her help.

My curiosity was especially piqued by a letter I found buried under a pile of papers. It was written by someone named Bessie Shields. Bessie Shields? Who was she? There was no salutation, so I was not sure to whom she was writing. The mysterious letter was fascinating. Bessie mentioned houses where family members lived, but provided no addresses—only descriptions of the homes and their locations. She wrote with assumed familiarity about "the little house on the corner" or the building "across from Uncle A.J."

I mentioned the letter to my sister Jean during our annual June family reunion at The Farm. This was Grandpa McKeon's place outside Fenton—the farm we had visited as kids. My grandfather, my dad, and my dad's brothers and sisters had been raised there. It's now a Centennial Farm and is still in the family.

I told Jean about Bessie Shields' letter. My idea was to go to Fenton, track down the houses she wrote about and take pictures of them. Jean was excited and agreed to begin the very next day.

That evening, I perused a family tree chart, hoping to find out more about Bessie. It turned out that she was Elizabeth Gould Shields, Granddad's half-sister. Their father was Judson Baylis Phillips. He and his half-brother, Andrew Jackson Phillips (A.J.), were prominent Fenton businessmen in the mid to late 1800s. The recipient of Bessie's letter was our grandmother's brother, Charles Judson Phillips, known as Juddy. Now I knew who Bessie was and how she was connected to the Phillips branch of my mother's family. It was an inspiring start to the adventure.

Jean and I met in downtown Fenton and parked near City Hall, thinking that might be a good place to begin our exploration. But before we got to the door an antique shop caught our attention. A boldly painted metal porch glider sitting out in front was reminiscent of the one Nonie and Gramp had on the patio at the cottage. It had to be a sign. Who could resist checking it out?

We made a quick detour to talk with the shop owner. To our delight, we discovered that we were standing in the building that had been the factory office for A.J. Phillips & Co. A.J.'s personal office was right next door. That building now housed the A. J. Phillips Historical Museum. We were standing smack dab in the middle of our family history.

The historical museum wasn't open, so we headed across the street to City Hall. The people there were eager to help: pulling out cemetery records and referring us to Ken Seeger at the historical museum and Doug Tabo at Oakwood Cemetery. We wrote those names down, made phone calls and met with both of them that afternoon. Then we learned that there was a Phillips family reunion planned for August. How opportune.

Finally, we were ready to begin our trek down Shiawassee Avenue. Map in one hand, Bessie's letter and camera in the other, we located the houses that had been built for A.J. Philips, Winfred Phillips, Harry Phillips and Ashley Phillips. No wonder Shiawassee had been called "Phillips' Row" by locals back in the day.

Peering at the map, gazing at the buildings and referring to the letter, we tried to identify which houses Bessie had referenced. We were fortunate to have a lot of additional information from the many photos, letters and cards from Dad's boxes.

What a feeling it was to stand in front of the house my great-grandparents Everett and Grace Scott bought as their "dream Victorian," to see our Granddad Clifford Phillips' house on Main Street which had been beautifully restored, and to see Uncle A.J.'s imposing mansion with the "mouse-proof walls" we had read about in a journal. The entire day was a walk back in time.

We saw the Presbyterian Church which Gramp attended as a child and St. Jude's Episcopal Church across the street where Nonie and her family worshiped. History really came alive as we recalled my grandfather's stories of watching Nonie play outside after services. He claimed he knew even as a boy that he was going to marry her.

Nonie and Gramp were both born in Fenton in 1906, just a few weeks apart. Nonie was born Nellie Geraldine Phillips and Gramp's full name was William Colwell Scott. Being from well-to-do families, both their mothers had a "helper girl," or nanny, when a baby was born. It happened that the helper girl for my grandfather and the helper girl for my grandmother were sisters. So on the day Nellie Phillips was born, little William Scott and his nanny went visiting. My grandmother and grandfather met as babies and literally knew each other their entire lives.

The stories in this book trace the history of the Phillips and Scott families, beginning in the mid-1800s and ending with Gramp and Nonie, who were in turn responsible for my early memories of the summer cottage and my lifelong fascination with all the buildings that held—and continue to hold—my family history.

# PART 2

## The Phillips

# Phillips Family Tree

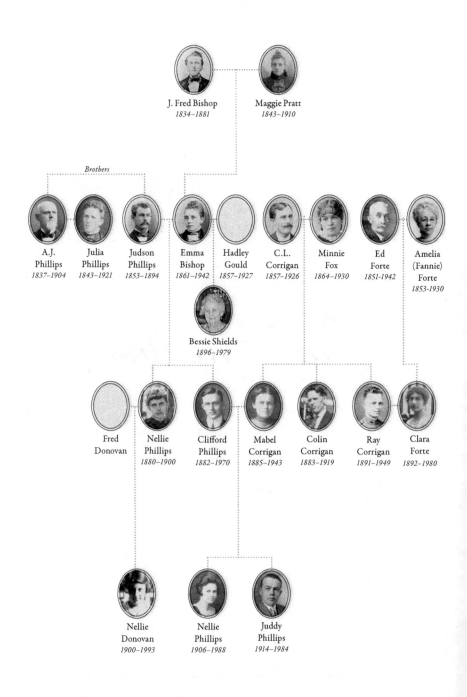

J. Fred Bishop
*1834–1881*

Maggie Pratt
*1843–1910*

*Brothers*

A.J.
Phillips
*1837–1904*

Julia
Phillips
*1843–1921*

Judson
Phillips
*1853–1894*

Emma
Bishop
*1861–1942*

Hadley
Gould
*1857–1927*

C.L.
Corrigan
*1857–1926*

Minnie
Fox
*1864–1930*

Ed
Forte
*1851-1942*

Amelia
(Fannie)
Forte
*1853-1930*

Bessie Shields
*1896–1979*

Fred
Donovan

Nellie
Phillips
*1880–1900*

Clifford
Phillips
*1882–1970*

Mabel
Corrigan
*1885–1943*

Colin
Corrigan
*1883–1919*

Ray
Corrigan
*1891–1949*

Clara
Forte
*1892–1980*

Nellie
Donovan
*1900–1993*

Nellie
Phillips
*1906–1988*

Juddy
Phillips
*1914–1984*

# 3

# The Courtship of Emma Bishop

"Emma! Emma Grace!" Mrs. Bishop called sharply as she rapped on the bedroom door. Without waiting for an answer, she impatiently turned the cut glass doorknob and walked in. Emma sat on the bed, looking miserable in her corset, petticoats and dressing gown. Eyes red and puffy from crying, her wire-rimmed glasses lay folded on the table beside her. The new ball gown hung forlornly in the wardrobe.

Maggie Bishop sighed. She felt for her daughter, but this would not do. Not tonight. "You are not dressed yet?" she scolded. "We need to leave."

Emma balled her embroidered linen handkerchief in her fist. "Oh, Mother! No, please. I cannot go!"

At only five feet tall, Maggie was small but spunky. She, too, was distraught at Gilbert's treatment of her daughter, but it was no use crying over spilt milk. Emma needed a strong hand now, not a shoulder to cry on.

"For heaven's sake, Emma!" she exclaimed. "This has gone on quite long enough. You have to go out eventually. You are sixteen years old. Do you intend to become an old maid, living with your father and me forever? You're much too pretty for that."

Emma shook her head in despair and wailed, "But Gilbert and I promised each other. We promised!"

"Gilbert's promise has obviously been broken. Rumor has it he's engaged to another, and a senator's daughter, at that. I'm sorry, my dear, but the sooner you accept the fact he's not returning for you the better off we all will be."

Maggie hoped that Emma would listen to reason. Everyone in town had heard the rumors of Gilbert's betrayal. Gilbert's mother had made sure of that. A slyly placed phrase in a letter, and a coy hint at another romance made it clear that she had orchestrated a more advantageous match for her son out west, without regard for the heart he'd broken back here.

Truth be told, Maggie was not terribly surprised at this turn of events. Gilbert's mother had always felt her family was above Fenton society. Maggie had warned Emma as much when Gilbert moved with his family to California. Such a social climber the woman was—good riddance to bad rubbish. Of course, far away in California, Gilbert and his mother were safely removed from the neighbor's gossip, stares and whispers when it became obvious that the engagement was broken. Poor Emma wasn't.

Maggie sighed again. She mustn't let this disappointment ruin her daughter's confidence. Perhaps a little compassion wouldn't hurt. Sitting on the bed next to Emma, Maggie took her daughter's hand. She smiled, attempting to be gentler. "You are young and beautiful, Emma. Many young men will be eager to court you."

Emma turned her tear-stained face up and pleaded, "But I don't want someone else. I want Gilbert. Please, don't make me go." She began to weep again.

*No,* thought Maggie. *I don't want to hurt you, dear, but I suppose I must be hard.*

Maggie let go of Emma's hand. She stood and shook her head, then walked to the dressing table where she poured water from a flowered ceramic pitcher into the matching bowl. She dipped a small towel into the bowl and wrung it out. Finally, she turned and handed the cloth to Emma. Her dark eyes were kind, but her voice was firm.

"We have tolerated your melancholy long enough," she stated with finality. "You will not miss the Knights Templar Ball tonight. I know you are wary of the gossip, but there will only be more talk if you do not make an appearance. Now don't let the wags see you this way. Here, wash your face."

Emma recognized that tone of voice and knew it well. The set of her mother's jaw said it all. There was no used arguing anymore. Resigned to her fate, the girl took the damp cloth and began to wipe her hot cheeks. Maggie continued.

"You will get dressed now, and go to the dance. You will smile and be utterly charming."

Emma managed a small smile and a hiccup slipped out.

"My dear daughter, the gossip will be over before you know it." Maggie's expression softened with affection for her daughter. "You are a Bishop. Remember that. And besides, that nice Mr. Phillips may be there."

Seeing the pained expression on her daughter's face, Maggie changed the subject. "We had better hurry. Your father already called for the carriage."

Emma stood up reluctantly, watching as her mother took the beautiful blue velvet gown off its hook. They both paused to admire its detail—small white ruffles along the neckline, puffed sleeves, lace at the wrist and the prominent bustle that Emma had declared to be "just darling!" The young woman had been thrilled when she and her mother ordered the dress months before. However, as the fittings progressed, Gilbert's letters had grown less frequent, finally stopping altogether. Emma grew less and less enthusiastic about the dress as the gossip started.

As she helped Emma dress, Maggie's thoughts turned to her own youth and gossip. She and Mr. Bishop had been so in love they had not stopped to consider the consequences of their passion. The timing was certainly poor. Frederick was about to begin law school when it became obvious their marriage could not wait. He became a grocer instead, and his family was furious.

Maggie loved her husband and was satisfied with her marriage and family. Likewise, Frederick had never uttered a word of disappointment at the turn his life had taken. Although he had been very successful, she still sometimes wondered how their life would have been different if Frederick had become an attorney.

While Emma smoothed the ruffles at her neckline, Maggie adjusted the bustle and straightened the draped fabric below it. Emma would survive the evening, Maggie told herself. Young people put such stock in love, but life had taught her that there was much more to be considered in a match. She knew that it was equally important to consider financial prospects and the family's standing in the community. But how does one convince a young girl that, over time, love is of little consequence?

Maggie straightened up and caught her daughter's eye in the mirror above the bureau. The tears were gone. She did look exquisite—putting on the gown seemed to have raised her hopes. Maggie did not want to dash those hopes with a lecture. Besides, how could she lecture Emma, given her own choices?

The Bishop's carriage took its place in the queue in front of the Masonic Temple. While they waited, Emma watched Milo Chapman, the village lamplighter, work his way down the street with his small ladder and torch, stopping at each lamppost. Mr. Chapman performed this duty every evening, but the ritual tonight seemed special somehow.

When it was their turn to disembark, the driver came round and took Emma's hand to help her alight. He then assisted her sister, Mary Louise, and Mrs. Bishop. Even though she felt beautiful in her new gown, Emma walked slowly and with a heavy heart behind her mother and father through the double doors that led upstairs to the ballroom. She missed Gilbert so and felt as if she was about to run a gauntlet.

Upstairs, a doorman held open the massive wooden door that led to the foyer. The family deposited their heavy coats and fur muffs there, then approached the large ballroom. Music filled the air as the guests mingled and talked. Inside, the opera seats had been moved and were lined up two deep around the sides of the entire floor. The stage had been decorated for the orchestra and the balcony cleared for spectators. Emma and her sister followed as their father escorted them into the ballroom. Out of habit, Emma opened her folding fan with a flick of her wrist, then decided that she would hide her face behind it all night. Filled with dread, she turned to her mother. "Is everyone looking at me?" she whispered anxiously.

"Emma, don't be a ninny!" chided Maggie in response. "No one of any importance gives a whit about your love life. Now go. Try to have a good time. Please."

And with that, her mother and father strode off, leaving Emma and Mary Louise standing alone. Emma furtively looked around, her face still hidden behind her fan. Could Mother be right? Maybe the gossip was dying down. No one had seemed to notice her entrance.

One person had, though—Judson Phillips, the man Emma's mother had referred to earlier. Standing in the balcony, he was positioned to have a good view of the entrance while watching the dancers glide around the floor. Relatively new in town, Judson had been working out west in the lumber industry when his half-brother A.J. suggested he join his thriving well pump business, hoping that Judson's energy and ingenuity would benefit the operation. Judson's arrival in Fenton had caused quite a stir. Many young ladies were anxious to make his acquaintance, but disappointment was to be their lot. Emma Bishop was the girl who had caught Judson's eye. In fact, being that he and his family were staunch Baptists, she was the only reason he was at the ball. It was her, and only her, he was hoping to see enter the ballroom that evening. Judson's face brightened when he saw the Bishops finally arrive. He quickly strode down the stairs to the main floor and across the room toward the young ladies.

"Emma. He's coming this way." whispered Mary Louise. "Look. Mr. Phillips."

"I'm very aware of Mr. Judson Phillips," sighed Emma. "I've heard enough about him, from you and all the other girls in town. I'm not interested. You know I'll always be true to Gilbert—"

"Hush up about old Gilbert." hissed Mary Louise.

In response, Emma flicked her fan open and turned away. Mary Louise frowned at her sister, then turned to Judson and flashed her sweetest smile.

"The Misses Bishop." he exclaimed. "So nice to see you tonight. I was beginning to think you were not coming."

Judson smiled at both girls, but his eyes traveled past Mary Louise to focus on Emma. Her naturally curly hair piled atop her head, her twinkling blue eyes, her high cheekbones—he was captivated. Emma surveyed him from behind her fan. Judson was a handsome man, she would give him that. He had a high forehead and deep, thoughtful eyes. His hair, parted on the side, was neatly combed back, cut straight above his ears. His large mustache, trim and waxed, was probably his most striking feature.

Their eyes met, but only for a moment. *What am I doing?* Emma said to herself, glancing down in embarrassment. *I will not be taken in by mere good looks.* She tried vainly to bring Gilbert's face to mind. Her darling Gilbert. Strangely, the face of her faraway love became blurry in her memory. Befuddled, Emma could only blush. She made no reply to Judson's greeting.

Fortunately, Mary Louise spoke up, "So nice to see you, too, Mr. Phillips. We're all so glad you've come to Fenton. And what do you think of our Knights Templar Ball?"

Judson looked around at the beautifully decorated ballroom, the throngs of people, the orchestra and the refreshments. "Truthfully," he said, "the stories I heard did not do it justice. This is something indeed."

Mary Louise smiled even more sweetly. "You are too kind. You've attended much grander balls in your travels, have you not?"

Judson didn't answer. He was staring at Emma.

Mary Louise's smile faded. Just her luck. The most handsome man in town seemed to be smitten with her sister. Well, maybe his attentions would get Emma's mind off Gilbert. She spoke again.

"Mr. Phillips?"

Judson took his eyes off Emma for a moment and shook his head. "Oh! My apologies, Miss Bishop. What were you saying?"

"Nothing important. Well, I must take my leave. I hope you enjoy the dancing."

"No, not me. I will be leaving when they start the Grand March. I don't dance. We're Baptist. But I certainly wouldn't have missed the opportunity to see all this."

"Well then, you and Emma are a match." Mary Louise laughed, despite the glare Emma shot at her. "My sister has the voice of a songbird. She gets it from Mother and our Welch ancestors. But she doesn't dance, either. No religious reason, just never learned!" And with that Mary flounced away, with a mischievous grin directed at Emma.

"That's a happy coincidence," Judson said to Emma. "That you don't dance, I mean. I came here hoping to speak to you tonight. May I call on you some time?"

"Oh, no!" Emma blurted out, louder than she meant to. She looked around quickly to see if anyone had overheard. Judson's frankness had surprised her, and she attempted to regain her composure. "That would not be proper, under the circumstances."

"Circumstances?" he asked. "What circumstances might those be?"

Emma felt her face flush again and raised her fan to cover the redness creeping up her neck and into her cheeks. Surely he had heard the rumors. He was toying with her.

"I am betrothed to another," she replied stiffly. "You must have heard. He is in California, but we intend to keep our promise."

"California, eh?" This information was not news to Judson, although he pretended it was. He had asked his sister-in-law, Julia, about Emma soon after he arrived in Fenton. Julia was a most reliable source for society information, and had told Judson the entire story.

"That is quite a distance," Judson remarked. "I myself have recently come from out west, working in the logging industry. What does your young man do in California?"

Emma pursed her lips and said nothing. She was embarrassed to admit that her beau was still in high school. He did seem rather young, now that she thought about it, especially compared to Judson.

Judson let the subject drop and continued to press his case. "Would it hurt to merely go out for a walk before you leave to join your fiancé? Perhaps a sleigh ride while we still have snow?"

Emma hesitated. She found Judson's offer tempting. Just a walk—it was harmless, wasn't it? And she did feel flattered. But what would Gilbert say if he knew? He loved her. She refused to even consider the awful rumor that Gilbert had found someone else. No, she had to stay true. Angry with herself that she had even considered accepting, Emma closed her fan with a snap and smacked it against her palm.

"Please, it would be better if you did not call," she said, averting her eyes from the young man's gaze.

Unaccustomed to being rebuffed, Judson was a bit surprised. Many of the young ladies in town had made it clear his attentions would be welcomed. He realized that winning Emma's affections would be a challenge. This fact made him even more determined to succeed at the game of love. Leaning in with steely resolve, Judson whispered in Emma's ear, "You and this young man? I daresay it's only puppy love. Goodnight, Miss Bishop."

Emma gasped in outrage. The words stung so sharply, she felt as if he'd slapped her. Before she could think of an answer, Judson was gone, having turned and walked quickly away. Hiding her face behind her fan, Emma scanned the room, although it was difficult without her spectacles. Had anyone witnessed their exchange?

Ah, there was Mary Louise, sidling up next to her. Her sister stood close to Emma and whispered severely. "You are a foolish, foolish girl!"

"You have no idea what you're talking about!" Emma insisted.

"Oh, I think I do. I saw Judson's face when he walked out the door."

Emma shrugged as if to say, "So what?"

Mary Louise held nothing back. "Gilbert is gone, Emma. He is most likely engaged to another and will not return for you."

Emma began to speak, but Mary Louise interrupted her protest. "Whether abandoning you was his idea or his mother's, the result is the same. Think about it, Emma. Would you really want such a mamma's boy?" Mary stopped her tirade to let her words sink in.

Emma was silent.

"Now, as for Judson Phillips," Mary continued, "He's from a good family and has excellent prospects."

Emma shrugged again.

"And he's a man, not a boy like Gilbert. A man knows what he wants and goes after it. Right now, Mr. Phillips seems to have his heart set on you. Most girls would be thrilled to be in your position. I know a few are jealous already, just from seeing him talk to you this evening."

"Really? The other girls are jealous?" asked Emma, smiling impishly.

Mary Louise smiled back. "Just keep an open mind—but don't wait too long, dear sister."

Riding home in the carriage, Emma pulled her wrap tightly around her shoulders. She had so been looking forward to this evening—her first Knights Templar Ball! But it had been a disaster. First, the rumors about Gilbert. Then, that rude Judson Phillips. Emma's head pounded. She was exhausted.

Wanting nothing more than to sink into bed and sleep, Emma was relieved to be home. However, as her mother and sister started upstairs, Mr. Bishop put his hand on his daughter's arm.

"Emma, come into my study. I'd like a word with you," he said.

Mary Louise looked at her with raised eyebrows but Emma shrugged, mystified as to why her father would need to speak with her. Had she done something wrong at the ball?

Mr. Bishop walked into the study, lit the gas lamp on his massive wooden desk, and motioned for his daughter to sit as he took his seat. She perched on the edge of a chair in front of the desk, her hands crossed on her lap.

"Your mother tells me you are still carrying a torch for Gilbert," he began. "Is this true?"

Emma flushed. Her father spoke again. "You don't need to answer, but I have something to say in this regard. Marriage is serious business, Emma. The man you choose impacts the rest of your life—where you will live, how well he can provide for you and your children, and if you will be happy."

Emma nodded. "I know, Father."

"So you must realize that you cannot trust this decision to a schoolgirl's crush. Your mother and I were lucky to be as compatible as we are. That is rare, but it happened because we thought long and hard before our betrothal. Please, do the same. I know you don't want to hear this, Emma, but Gilbert and his family have shown their true colors. You may think this is just a doting father's opinion, but Gilbert does not deserve your love and loyalty."

Emma dropped her head. She was a bit embarrassed at her father's words, but knew he spoke from love.

Mr. Bishop opened a desk drawer and pulled out a small box "I want you to have this," he said. "It has long been in my family. You know, when your mother and I were married, our families were not at all happy. They wanted me to study law and become an attorney. But my grandmother gave me this ring. She explained there were more important things to consider and she could see that your mother and I would complement each other."

He stood, walked around the desk to Emma, opened the blue cloth-covered box and handed it to her. Inside was a delicate ring of gold and silver bands twisted together.

"This ring is called a lover's knot," he explained. "The silver and gold strands are separate, yet intertwined they make a beautiful whole. Marriage is like that. You don't need to wear it—just keep it somewhere safe. When you consider a mate, think about this ring. Can the man you choose complete your lover's knot?"

"Father, I do so want the man to be Gilbert," Emma admitted. "But I will keep the ring in mind."

Emma was resting in her room the next afternoon when her mother came in and announced that Judson Phillips was down in the parlor.

"Oh, Mother, please," She sat up quickly and scrambled for an excuse. "Tell him I'm not seeing visitors, tell him I'm not well, tell him I'm out."

"I will do no such thing!" answered Mrs. Bishop. "He's making a formal call and I'll not have you treat him rudely. You must mind your manners, young lady."

Emma slumped back on her chaise. She knew her mother was right. It would not do for her to be impolite. Sighing, she stood and straightened her dress, gave a quick look in her hand mirror, smoothed her hair and pinched her cheeks for some color. Her thoughts raced as she primped. Why would he be paying a call? She thought she had made it clear his attentions were not welcome.

Emma could see Judson standing in the parlor as she followed her mother down the stairs. She had to admit that he looked quite dapper in his day suit, bowler hat in hand, like any proper gentleman. A man, and a very handsome one at that. Her heart skipped. A week ago she would have assumed he was here to see her father, but today he was here to see her. She thought about last night. Had Judson really done anything untoward? Emma's stomach soured a little. Maybe it was her behavior that was unfortunate. Suddenly, she felt chagrined and uncertain.

Emma paused at the parlor door, unsure how to proceed. Judson noticed her and smiled broadly.

"Hello, Mr. Phillips. I—I do apologize if I was unnecessarily brusque last night," she stammered.

"Not at all, Miss Bishop. It is I who was in the wrong," said Judson, his smile becoming softer. "I came to apologize for my conduct last night. I should not have doubted your young man's intentions. My behavior was absolutely boorish."

Mrs. Bishop motioned for Judson to sit, but he shook his head. "No, thank you. I merely intended a short call. I will leave my card at the door." With that, he nodded to mother and daughter, donned his hat and walked out.

Emma was speechless.

So was her mother. "What in the world—" she began, dying to know the circumstances behind the young man's apology. She decided not to press the matter when Emma rushed from the room, holding back tears.

After that day, Emma was more confused than ever. She had not heard from Gilbert for several months. As much as she did not want to believe that he was engaged to another girl, she finally acknowledged that the rumors might be true. Admitting this to herself didn't hurt as much as she thought it would.

Soon, Emma found herself thinking of her old love less and less—and Judson more and more. She began to hope that he would call again.

But he did not. Emma began to socialize with Mary Louise and their friends. She looked for Judson at every event, but there was no chance encounter. She told herself it didn't matter. Several other young men had become quite attentive. She didn't need Mr. Judson Phillips.

However, Emma often caught herself looking for him when she ran errands for her mother. She volunteered to walk to the post office to collect the mail, hoping their paths would cross. She seldom thought of Gilbert as spring turned into summer and summer dragged on.

"I think our Emma is recovering. You know, out of sight, out of mind," Mrs. Bishop spoke confidentially to Mary Louise one morning.

"Maybe Gilbert is out of sight, out of mind," Mary Louise whispered back. "But not Mr. Judson Phillips!"

Her mother looked at her in surprise. "Whatever do you mean?"

"Oh, Mother! You haven't noticed when we go out? Emma is always looking around like she's lost something. Now who do you think she's looking for?"

"Mr. Phillips?"

"Most certainly. And he seems to have disappeared."

~~~~~~~~~~~~~~~~~~~~~~~~~~~~~~

By August, preparations were underway for the annual Pioneer Picnic, held out by Woodhull's Landing on Lake Fenton. Everyone in town would be there, and Emma was determined to see Judson. She had been saving her new paisley print summer dress just for this occasion. It had a high neck, wide lapels with a row of shiny buttons between them, fitted sleeves slightly puffed at the shoulder, and a straight, slim skirt—the newest fashion.

The day of the picnic was beautiful, with the sun shining on the water and a gentle breeze coming off the lake. A few boats were out practicing for the races, their bright white sails flashing against the blue of the waves and sky. Emma and Mary Louise carried Chantilly lace parasols as they strolled with their parents through a sea of large bobbing flowered hats. Mary Louise squeezed Emma's hand when she noticed her sister anxiously glancing to and fro.

"I'll keep an eye out for him, too," she said in a sympathetic whisper.

The family found seats in front of the bandstand to listen to the program.

Emma tried to pay attention, but found the speeches more than a trifle boring: politicians extolling the virtues of the Pioneers back when Fenton was called Dibbleville, and how Mr. LeRoy, Mr. Horton, and Mr. Fenton had wagered for the naming rights to the village in a game of poker. She knew this history all too well, Grandma Pratt being a Dibble and all.

It was actually Emma's father who spotted Judson when the family stood to leave after the speeches. Mr. Bishop called out a greeting. Judson turned towards them and nodded. He excused himself from a girl he had been talking to and strolled over. The girl, who Emma did not recognize, giggled and walked away.

Mr. Bishop enthusiastically shook Judson's hand. "Mr. Phillips. How nice to see you. I believe you've met Mrs. Bishop and my daughters, Miss Emma Bishop and Miss Mary Louise Bishop?"

Judson tipped his straw boater. "Yes, indeed. We spoke at the Knights Templar Ball last winter when I was still fairly new in town. They made me feel most welcome."

The men chatted for a few minutes. Emma stood there silently, feeling awkward. Judson hadn't even said hello! Well, why should he? She had missed her chance. After all this time, he was probably courting someone else. Emma cleared her throat, trying to think of a way to excuse herself. Just then, Judson turned to face her.

"Would you like to take a walk around the picnic grounds?"

Surprised and excited, Emma's face colored. She looked at her father for permission.

He nodded his approval. "Just meet us back for lunch."

Judson offered Emma his arm, and she nervously placed her hand in the crook of his elbow. She was suddenly acutely aware of their age difference. Gilbert had been a schoolboy. Judson, with his gentlemanly manner, well-tailored clothes and handsome mustache, was a man.

The couple strolled through the crowded park, enjoying the festive atmosphere. The Fenton Village band had set up and was breezily playing "The Man on the Flying Trapeze." Several boys raced by, pushing barrel hoops with sticks. Judson gently steered Emma out of their way. A badminton net had been erected and two young couples were beginning a game.

Emma waited for Judson to strike up a conversation, but he only looked down and smiled at her now and then as they walked. Finally, she blurted out, "I'm surprised I haven't seen you around this summer. Have you been back out west?"

He paused, then answered slowly, looking into the distance. "No. I'll admit I've been avoiding you. You made it clear last winter that you were spoken for."

Abruptly, Judson stopped walking. He turned and stared hard at Emma, searching her face. "I find that Fenton suits me quite well. I plan to stay here. And you, Emma? Do you have plans to travel west?"

*Such a simple question,* thought Emma. And yet it wasn't. It held a great deal of meaning for both her and Judson. She hesitated, fully aware of what her answer would imply.

Standing in the middle of the noisy picnic grounds and looking up at Judson Phillips' serious expression, Emma felt as if she were standing at a crossroads. She was no longer a girl, but was she prepared to be a woman? This man was strong and handsome. As her mother and sister said, he had good prospects. He also seemed kind and intelligent. Was he the other half of her lover's knot? Would there be another chance if she turned him away again? Emma made her decision. When she spoke, she was sure of her answer. "No. I have no plans to travel. I agree with you, Judson. Fenton is where I belong, too."

Judson's expression relaxed into the gentle smile Emma would come to know and love. He took both her hands and pulled her close for a moment. She could feel the warmth of his chest on the back of her hands, and it made her shiver—a funny tingling feeling that she didn't know what to make of. Emma was quite puzzled by her feelings. She felt nervous and excited but also safe and content. *Maybe Mother can explain it,* she thought. *I'll ask her later.* The band broke into "The Sidewalks of New York" as Judson and Emma resumed their walk.

Judson was also struggling with a myriad of emotions. He could hardly believe this fortunate turn of events. After the Knights Templar Ball the previous winter, he had asked his sister-in-law, Julia, for advice. Consulting her copy of "The Essential Handbook of Edwardian Etiquette," Julia instructed Judson to make a formal apology and not pursue Emma any further.

Discouraged in love, Judson threw himself into work whole-heartedly. He had many ideas for improvements to his brother's business, and it grew quickly. Orders came in from all over the country, keeping Judson busy and giving him a good excuse to ignore the flirtations of several young women in the village. He knew the caliber of woman he wanted for his wife. No one but Emma measured up. But how could he win her? Following Julia's advice, Judson simply waited, hoping Emma would eventually be free.

Now—finally—she was, and she seemed to reciprocate his affection. Judson pressed Emma's arm tightly against his side. He could feel his heart thumping hard in his chest. They walked in happy silence for a few minutes.

Judson had so much he wanted to say to Emma, but he feared it was too soon. When he spoke again he talked of work. "We're running double shifts at the factory with over 200 men. Orders are coming in like hotcakes. The Grand Trunk Railroad has agreed to run a spur over to the factory to handle our freight."

Emma nodded in admiration. Her father had said that A. J. Phillips & Co was the future of Fenton. The city fathers had even voted to give a stipend to Judson's brother, A.J., to expand the factory. Many people said that Judson was the genius behind the patents and machinery used in the factory. Emma felt proud to be walking by his side.

As they returned to meet her family for lunch, Judson stopped. He turned to Emma and asked, "May I call on you again?"

She smiled and nodded.

# 4
# Julia Phillips, Matriarch

1883

Home of A.J. and Julia Phillips. Photo courtesy of A J Phillips Historical Museum

Julia Phillips looked out the front bay window as her sister-in-law Emma walked back across the muddy ruts of Shiawassee Avenue to her own home. She could certainly see why Judson had been attracted to Emma. She was pretty, graceful, and had a sweet disposition. Julia shook her head and gave an audible "tsk" as she watched Emma open the door of the modest two-story frame house and disappear inside. Why Judson and Emma continued to live there was beyond her. She would admit that the wraparound porch and signature red window were charming, but the house certainly wasn't large enough to entertain properly. And they needed the room, now that their family had grown.

As the undisputed matriarch of the Phillips clan, Julia felt it her obligation to guide her family in the right direction. More than once, she had suggested to Judson that he build a new, larger home, befitting his station. There were several large lots right here on the Avenue! To Julia's dismay, however, the couple seemed quite content in their little white house.

She let the velvet drapery drop and turned back to the dimly lit parlor, her frown relaxing. Julia had very capable features: a strong nose, firm lips and a set jaw. Recently, she had taken to wearing small rimless eyeglasses. Her grey hair was softly pulled back and swept up into a neat bun.

Julia sat at the tea table to pour herself another cup. She was fond of Emma and enjoyed their daily visits over a cup of tea but, due to their age difference, considered her more a daughter than a sister-in-law. In that capacity, she was happy to advise Emma when it came to menu planning, shopping, and supervising the help. After all, Julia had been running her own large household for years. She had even bought Emma a copy of "Mrs. Beeton's Book of Household Management," which she considered a requirement for any young wife.

Despite Julia's best efforts, however, Emma simply did not have a head for figures. Marrying so young put her at quite a disadvantage. Her beauty and charm had caused Judson to fall in love with her, but it had not prepared Emma to run a household.

To Julia's frustration, this did not seem to bother Judson. Outside of the small weekly allowance he gave his wife, he personally took care of the majority of the household expenses. He even traveled to Detroit on shopping excursions for clothes for Emma, little Nellie and baby Clifford.

Julia frowned again. Most unusual. She would never tolerate such behavior from her husband. A.J. would never suggest it, thankfully. The two had come to an understanding early in their union. She ran the household and A.J. handled the business. Julia was proud of his success. The small operation had long since expanded from producing only well pumps and had grown until it was one of the largest manufacturers in the entire state!

A.J. wasn't perfect in every area of their marriage, however. Julia didn't approve of his drinking and card playing. Apparently A.J. was only a "Sunday Baptist." Even so, she would never dream of meddling in his business affairs.

The same was true for the household. That was Julia's domain, and the men in her family knew full well not to interfere. If only she could convince Emma to take charge at home. After all, what other choice was there for a woman?

The maid was hovering nearby. Julia motioned for her to clear the tea things, then decided to send a message to Judson at the office. During their tea, Emma had mentioned little Nellie's bad cough. Should she call Dr. Gould? Or was there a home remedy she should try? The answer was simple, Julia said, trying to calm the young mother's worries. Dr. Collis Browne's chlorodyne pills were the answer, of course.

Emma would probably forget, however. Julia sat at her writing desk and took up pen and paper. She would make sure Judson stopped at the druggist this afternoon.

# 5
## Summer Fun

1893

Summers were great. That was the only word for it! After their chores were done, Clifford and his friends spent their days playing baseball, skittles, riding their bicycles. Often they went swimming off the bridge over the Shiawassee River, and sometimes they just explored. If there were enough participants, they would re-enact the Indian Conflicts out west. Wielding sticks and toy guns, the battles were hard fought. The inevitable cuts and bruises were worn with pride.

As evening approached, Clifford looked forward to stopping by the offices of A.J. Phillips & Co, to walk his father home for supper. Clifford's father, Judson, worked in the business office on Leroy Street, a handsome wooden building with a Mansard roof. Beyond the office were the brick warehouses and the factory. The warehouses were three stories tall and connected to the factory by an elevated tramway running across the mill. Clifford loved to watch the tram, loaded with supplies, swing slowly across the mill.

Down on the factory floor, the men were busy

Clifford Phillips—age 9

making all sorts of household products: ironing boards, snow shovels, washboards, clothesline poles, wagon jacks, step ladders, lawn swings, hammocks—just about anything you could think of. The whirr of saw blades and the clean smell of freshly cut wood filled the air. Clifford marveled at the process from start to finish. It was fascinating. He knew his father had an important job, creating the designs for the machines and the products. But he thought the real action was on the factory floor.

Arriving at the building, Clifford walked up the wooden steps and across the porch to the office. The screen door creaked as he pulled it open, stretching the thin wire spring. The door snapped shut behind him. Clifford was allowed to visit his father at work, but only if he did not disturb anyone. He pulled off his cap and politely sat on the wooden bench in the reception area.

It was quiet in the business office. The pendulum in the wall clock ticked off the final minutes of the work day. The click of a typewriter's keys from behind a closed door, and the murmur of muffled voices in an office down the hall were all that disturbed the silence, until Clifford's uncle A.J. emerged from the front office. An intimidating-looking man, A.J. had a bulbous nose, white hair fringing his bald head and a neatly trimmed beard beneath a thin mouth. He wore a three-piece suit with four-in-hand-tie. Spotting his nephew, A.J. slapped him on his shoulder heartily.

"Hey, young fellow. I thought I heard you come in."

A.J. enjoyed time with Clifford, since his own boys were older. Harry was still in high school, but Winfield and Ashley were already grown men. They handled sales for the factory. Grinning at Clifford, Uncle A.J. leaned against the door frame and fished around in his suit pocket. After a moment, he pulled out a licorice drop and handed it to Clifford.

As Clifford chewed on the candy, his uncle sat down next to him on the bench and whispered loudly, "I hear you might get a special treat this weekend."

Clifford sat up a little straighter. "A treat! What is it, Uncle A.J.?"

"Oh, I don't want to spoil the surprise," he chuckled. I'm sure your father will tell you when he's ready."

A.J. pulled out his pocket watch, glanced at it and then up at the wall clock. Right on cue, the whistle mounted high on the warehouse blew, signaling the end of the work day.

Clifford's father came out of his office, smiling when he saw his young son. He put his hat on his head, picked up his fashionable cane with the ivory handle and nodded to A.J. Clifford donned his cap as well, trying to emulate his father's easy, polished manner. He wished he had a walking stick, too. As father and son walked the two blocks home, Clifford could hardly contain his excitement. He couldn't wait to hear about the big surprise for the weekend. But his father didn't mention it.

Instead, Judson remarked, "I heard you got into a little scrape the other day, in front of the Rose's house."

Clifford was taken aback. How did father know about that? *I bet that stinker Billy Rose snitched,* he thought. *I'm pretty sure this is the end of the weekend surprise.*

The boy hung his head as he spoke. "It was nothing, really," he began. "We didn't fight or anything. Billy Rose was just bragging about Rose Manufacturing being the whip socket capital of the world and how smart his father is. I wasn't going to stand for that. I told him Rose Manufacturing was no great shakes. whip sockets. How can he even compare that to the Phillips factory? Look at all the things in your catalogue."

Clifford's voice rose as he continued to press his case. "Father, you sell in all forty-four states, and Europe, and—and—even Australia. I told Billy so. I told him you even put the new screen windows in the White House for the president. That knocked him off his high horse. Then he ran inside, to tell his mother, I guess."

Judson kept a stern face during his son's speech, but inside he was laughing. It wasn't a punishable offense, after all. Old Mrs. Rose certainly had the reputation of being a busybody, sitting in her picture window watching over the neighborhood with opera glasses, only too eager to report a boy to his parents no matter how minor the scuffle was. Didn't every town have one?

His father didn't respond to the story. Clifford hoped that maybe he wasn't in trouble after all. Anyway, he couldn't wait any longer for the answer to his question. "So do I still get the treat this weekend that Uncle A.J. told me about?" he asked hopefully.

Judson chuckled, "Well, since I've already promised your mother and Nellie, I suppose so. I thought we'd go out on Lake Fenton for the day. What do you say to that?" Clifford nodded eagerly. He couldn't think of anything he'd like better.

Saturday morning was hot and sunny. Judson, Emma, Nellie and Clifford all walked over to Eddy's stables across from the Fenton Hotel, with Judson carrying the large wicker picnic basket. Mr. Eddy, who everyone called "Captain," had an old narrow-gauge railroad car which ran on tracks that traveled the two miles out to Lake Fenton. His horse was blind, but she could pull that trolley car along the cinder path and never trip over the railroad ties.

"Better'n most man or horse with sight," Captain Eddy would brag. Sometimes, however, if the car was overloaded, the conductor had to hop out and push to get them started.

During the ride to the lake, Clifford thought of the ships they would see at the docks. "Which boat will we take?" he asked his father excitedly, tugging on his sleeve.

Horse drawn trolley to Lake Fenton. Photo courtesy of A J Phillips Historical Museum

Two huge steamboats, each capable of holding over 600 passengers, dominated the lakeshore: the "City of Fenton," owned by Captain Eddy, and the "City of Flint," owned by his rival, Captain Foster. Captain Eddy and Captain Foster had a long-running feud. Who had the faster ship? Who would get the most passengers? They competed by slashing fares and sometimes hiring the Fenton Ladies' Band to play on board. The rivalry was fun to watch.

Judson preferred the smaller boats: the "Maccabee," the "Belle of the Lake," and the "Genesee Chief." These held only 200 passengers, but were able to dock at Case's Island. When the trolley stopped at Lake Fenton, the "Belle of the Lake" was just getting up a head of steam. Clifford's father chose her, and the family boarded as it prepared to shove off.

They paid the fare, 20 cents each, and found their seats. Emma and Nellie stayed on the first level to be out of the sun, but Clifford scrambled up on the top deck. He loved the view of the boat gliding away from the pier, accompanied by the gentle chop of the waves against the hull and the engine noise droning in the background.

Clifford hung over the rail watching as they passed Bay Port's newly constructed hotel and then the three-story diving platform at Johnson's Landing. The "Belle" steamed past Woodhull Landing, then Log Cabin Point, so named for the huge log cabin being built there with turrets, balconies and stone chimneys. At Summit Heights, a three-story pavilion had been erected with facilities for water-tobogganing, swimming and boating. There was even a huge water slide.

Soon, Case's Island came into view. The captain cut the power, threw the engine into reverse and the "Belle" slowed as it approached the landing area. The crew grabbed the wooden posts as they pulled up alongside the pier, then secured the "Belle" with ropes. A small wooden gangplank was set into place. The captain stood at the end of the gangplank, offering his hand as the passengers disembarked.

City of Flint on Lake Fenton. Photo courtesy of the A J Phillips Historical Museum

Once on shore, it was a short uphill walk up to the large park on the island. Picnic tables and towering trees dotted the grassy expanse of the park. Rustic frame cottages ran single file the length of the island. A hand pump provided water from a cool, deep well. Emma chose a table under a shady oak. She and Nellie began to unload the picnic basket while Clifford ran to hop on the swing.

The swing was the most wonderful thing on the island. Suspended between two tall trees, the huge platform swing had two levels and could hold so many children that no one ever had to wait a turn. Given its size, it swung slowly, so any latecomers could easily jump on board. Clifford never tired of looking up to see up to how the swing was attached. A wooden pole was secured high up between two very tall trees. Two wide metal bands wrapped around the pole and attached to wooden planks that ran down and attached to the swing platform. Just looking up at the amazing contraption took Clifford's breath away.

Too soon, Nellie called for Clifford to wash his hands at the well pump and come eat lunch. He only realized how hungry he was when he saw his mother unwrap the fried chicken and buttered biscuits. After finishing off his second slice of cherry pie, Clifford jumped up, ready to run and play again. His mother warned him not to hop back on the swing so soon after eating, so Clifford walked down the worn path to the far end of the island while his lunch settled. He could look across the narrows to the woods on Crane's Pointe, so close he could swim there if he'd wanted to.

Fenton Bicycle Club

Several hours later, the "Belle" returned for the trip home. Back on the top deck, Clifford spotted Captain Westcott's sailboat, the "Who Would Have Thought It," practicing for a race. His wasn't the most modern boat, but he was rarely beaten. Clifford waved as they passed. He also kept a lookout for a glimpse of the Wheelman's Club of Flint. It was exciting to see the men on their high wheel bikes racing on the cinder trail along the lake. All in all, it had been a great day.

# 6

## A Young Girl's Fancy

### 1893

Clifford's older sister, Nellie, loved to look across the street at Uncle A.J. and Aunt Julia's huge beautiful home. Solidly built and a full three stories, it was most certainly the largest house in the village. Uncle A.J. boasted that it was mouse-proof. He had 2 x 4's laid flat on top of each other in all the walls to make them especially solid. Nellie's father said that Uncle A.J. must really hate mice. She laughed at the thought.

Mouse-proof or not, Nellie thought the house was absolutely grand. The portico over the wide front steps was decorated in gold relief and the double-wide front doors bore etched glass windows. A wide porch wrapped around the front and sides of the house. It was perfect for sipping lemonade or cold tea while sitting in one of the wooden rockers.

The second floor held the bedrooms. One of the bedrooms facing the avenue had a balcony, the other a bay window. How Nellie wished her bedroom had a balcony! Wouldn't that be divine?

The third floor was the ballroom, which featured a beautifully polished floor and lovely draperies. Nellie's favorite feature of the house was the three small windows in the ballroom, bowing in under an arched medallion which was also in gold relief. She had never seen anything like it.

Rich wood paneling, massive doors and elaborate built-in cabinets lent a sense of elegance to the entire house. Nellie thought the pass-through serving window from the kitchen to the dining room was very clever. There was even indoor plumbing with wash basins in every bedroom!

Uncle A.J. and Aunt Julia entertained often. Nellie loved to stand at her little red front window to watch the carriages pull up and the ladies and gentlemen alight. The men wore their finest frock coats with silk-faced lapels, matching vests, finely checked trousers, wing collared shirts and wide ties. Many sported mutton-chop whiskers. The ladies' elaborate evening dresses had low, round necklines embellished with ribbons and flowers and enormous mutton sleeves topped with bows.

But the hats were Nellie's favorite. In the summer, the ladies wore straw boaters with birds' wings, bright flowers and feathers. In the winter the hats were wool or velvet, with ostrich plumes and flowers. All the hats were huge. It seemed to Nellie that the ladies tried to outdo each other. Did the biggest hat win a prize or something? Her papa joked, "Woe to any man stuck sitting behind one of those hats at Colwell's Opera House."

Music played long into the night during Aunt Julia's parties. In the summer, with the windows open, Nellie could hear the tunes wafting through the warm air as she lay in bed, drifting off to sleep to "My Darling Clementine" or "After the Ball."

The morning after an event at the big house, Nellie's mother would tell her all about the party: what food was served, who was there, what they wore and what exciting news was discussed. Nellie heard about the murder trial of Lizzie Borden and the World Columbian Exposition in Chicago. It was said the exposition had a Ferris wheel 264 feet tall that could hold over 2,000 people at one time. Emma described the Tiffany Chapel—the largest glass enclosed area in the world. What a wonderful sight it must be.

At nearly thirteen years of age, Nellie could hardly wait until she was old enough to attend the parties. Imagining herself dressed in the finest velvet and silk, she gazed in her mirror, often critically. Studying her reflection, she decided her ears stuck out a little too far and her face was too full for her liking. Oh, well. Most girls became prettier as they got older, didn't they? The clothes her father brought back from his trips to Detroit were beautiful, anyway. Nellie would be beautiful too, when she came of age. At least she hoped so.

# 7
## A Sad Decoration Day

MAY 1894

Spring cleaning was finally completed. Emma surveyed the gleaming wood-work and sparkling crystal chandeliers. The freshly laundered lace curtains fluttered in the spring breeze and the scent of blooming lilacs wafted in. It had been a long, cold, snowy winter, typical for Michigan. Eager to rid the house of the grimy layer of coal dust which covered everything, she had been so glad when they could finally open the windows and start the work.

Emma supervised as the house girls took each room completely apart. They beat the rugs out on the clothesline, washed the windows, scrubbed the floors, and replaced the winter curtains with the summer ones. The process took several weeks, but when they were done, the entire house smelled fresh and clean.

Emma had hoped that cleaning and airing out the house would improve her husband's health but, to her dismay, he grew noticeably worse. His coughing never seemed to end, and his chest was so sore he had trouble sitting comfortably. Judson was tired in the morning and even more tired at the end of the day. Emma spent many afternoons with Julia, her sister-in-law, who did her best to comfort the young mother.

After a hushed conversation with Dr. Jefferson Gould during his last visit, Emma realized there was nothing more he could do. Consumption. What a terrible word. It did indeed seem as if the disease was consuming poor Judson's body, making him weaker by the day. Emma tried to keep the children away from their father's sickbed, but she couldn't hide her rising grief from them. Clifford and Nellie became quiet and pensive.

One morning a few days later, Judson seemed particularly bad. His skin was ashen. The sunken cheeks and dark circles under his hooded eyes frightened Emma. He had aged so much over the last year! As Emma entered the bedroom with an extra wool blanket, Judson tried to speak. He could barely get the words out between coughing fits. "Emma, I need to talk to you," he gasped through dry, cracked lips.

Emma felt her chest tighten. Dreading what Judson was going to say, she put the blanket on the end of the bed and sat next to him, taking his hand in hers. Her husband's touch still made her feel safe and loved.

"You know what Dr. Gould told us," Judson began, fighting back a cough. "My health is not likely to get better and I'm afraid it's not long now. I worry about you and the children when I'm gone. We have to talk about this."

Tears pooled in Emma's eyes. She didn't want to think about what he was saying. She just wanted to stay in this moment, here, with him. Unable to look at Judson, she stood and walked to the folding sink. How many mornings she had watched him at that sink doing his daily ablutions?

Emma couldn't help smiling to herself. Judson had been intrigued when he first heard about an indoor sink. He ordered one from the Folding Bath Tub Co. in Marshall, Michigan, wondering if it was something they could adapt and manufacture at the factory. They were amazed when it was delivered. The sink stood tall in a wooden cabinet. Water was poured into a reservoir via an opening at the top behind a mirror. With the sink folded down, water could be poured into it by turning a handle called a faucet. When you were finished, the water emptied into another holding chamber. There was storage for Judson's shaving cream and brush, and even a drawer that pulled out for his shoe shine brushes and waxes.

Emma shook herself back to reality. She carefully turned the faucet, filled the copper sink basin, and moistened one of Judson's handkerchiefs. She walked back to the bed and brushed the hair off her husband's forehead, then ran the cold cloth along his brow and kissed him gently. "Please Juddy, let's not—"

Judson interrupted her with what little strength he could muster. "Emma, if not now, when? I've put this off long enough. I should have done more to prepare you. We—we have to talk now."

It was true. Emma was not prepared to live alone. Judson had always handled everything. She kept the weekly household money he gave her in a blue Mason jar in the kitchen cupboard. This was for milk and eggs and small household expenses. When they needed anything else, Juddy took care of it.

Emma turned away. A tear came to her eye as she recalled his extravagant shopping trips to Detroit. He would return with elegant gowns for her, dresses and shoes for Nellie, knickers and shirts for Clifford, and once, even a little cowboy outfit! He was such a wonderful husband and father. To think that she had been such a young, foolish girl that she almost hadn't married him. Emma turned back and gazed at her husband, once hale and hearty, now thin and haggard, wasting away from consumption. How could this be happening?

Judson spoke again, wringing the last from his small burst of energy. "Emma,

I've set up trusts for the children. When they turn twenty-one, they will receive their inheritance. I've asked Win to handle the finances for you."

Emma caught her breath, shocked, as she heard this news. She and Judson had never argued, and she didn't want to disagree with him now. But the thought of Win in charge of their affairs worried her. There was something about Judson's nephew that Emma didn't trust.

"Juddy, no! Not Win! If you don't think I can handle it, then let Ashley be the one. I am not going to go begging to Winfield for every last nickel and dime. Please reconsider."

Judson didn't answer. He held the white linen handkerchief to his mouth, consumed by another coughing fit, the longest yet. When he took it away, she could see the bloody phlegm. He lay back against the pillow and closed his eyes.

"I've always marveled that I was finally able to win your heart, Emma. You know I'd do just about anything for you." He reached for her hand. "But this is business, and I'm not going to argue about it." His breath rattled. "We need a good businessman. I've chosen Win." He choked back a cough. "I know he will do right by you and the children." By now Judson's voice was barely audible. "Julia will see to that."

Emma felt as if her world was crumbling around her, but she had to stay strong. Setting aside thoughts of her bleak future, she rose to get a clean handkerchief for Judson. Suddenly, the sound of voices and music outside the open window distracted her. *What in the world?* She walked to the window and pulled the curtain aside. She saw crowds lining Shiawassee and heard the firemen's band play the opening bars to a John Phillip Sousa march. Voices called out below, merrily greeting each other. Finally, it dawned on Emma that today was Decoration Day. The parade was forming for the march to Oakwood Cemetery, where the townspeople would pay their respects to the fallen soldiers. Emma's eyes filled with tears. *Didn't they know? Talking, laughing, music—how could they at a time like this?* She slammed down the sash and turned away.

# 8
## Life Without Father

1898—1900

A shadow descended on the lives of Emma and her children the first few years after Judson died. Already a quiet boy, Clifford maintained a perpetually sad look—his eyes dull, his mouth grim, his hair shorn close to his head. Both his mother and his Aunt Julia worried about him. Nellie left home to attend college in Ann Arbor, and Julia suggested Clifford be sent to the Orchard Lake Military Academy. She thought the change of scenery, plus the military discipline, would be good for him. Emma was reluctant to lose the company of both her children, but she agreed.

At first, Clifford didn't care much where he went to school. Being away from home helped get his mind off his father's death, however, and he found that he liked the Academy. The boys there were good pals. They practiced marching and went camping in addition to their studies. Clifford even won an honor for a poem he wrote about a soldier in the Spanish-American War. As busy as he was, though, he still missed home and looked forward to returning in the spring.

Nellie also came home in May, bringing with her a bad cough. Emma was distraught. "It sounds just like Judson's cough!" she told Julia. "She's only eighteen. I am taking no chances with my daughter." Julia agreed, and Emma called Dr. Jefferson Gould immediately.

After Dr. Gould examined Nellie, he shook his head sadly. "I'm afraid it is consumption," he said. "But it is not in an advanced stage as yet. The best course is to send her somewhere warm to recuperate."

Judson hadn't heeded the advice to rest in a warm climate, but the doctor hoped Emma would listen to him for Nellie's sake. Luckily, Emma had an artist friend named Mina K. Boothe who lived in Florida. They arranged for Nellie to stay with her.

Miss Boothe invited Clifford as well, and he agreed to go. Life at home had become even more difficult for him. Dr. Jefferson Gould's brother, Hadley Gould, had been courting Emma. Clifford kept his thoughts to himself. He knew his mother would most likely remarry but did not warm to the idea of another man taking his father's place in their family. He was glad to get away.

Happily, the Florida weather did wonders for Nellie's health. She regained enough strength to resume her studies and began attending Stetson University. She also played the organ at her church.

One afternoon, Nellie sat at the church organ, practicing a few hymns. Florida was hot, and a side door was propped open to catch any small breeze that might find its way in. The bright sun filtered through the stained glass windows, creating a kaleidoscope of colors on Nellie's sheet music and the keyboard. She ignored the play of lights, intent on getting the tempo of the song just right. Sometimes the choir tended to slow the hymns down to a snail's pace. It ruffled her feathers. As she practiced, beads of sweat trickled down her back and the thin cotton of her dress clung uncomfortably.

During a pause in the music, the creak of the floorboards startled Nellie. She looked up, seeing the silhouette of a man off to the side of the choir vestry.

"I didn't want to disturb you. You seemed so intent," he said.

Nellie squinted to see him better in the shadows of the nave. He sounded young, and from his outline she could tell he was tall and slender.

"I'm the new assistant preacher," he said, taking a few steps forward. "Frederick Donovan." His voice was rich and melodious. "I've just been assigned to this parish. You must be Nellie Phillips, the organist. I was told I'd find you here."

Nellie slid off the wood bench seat and walked to him. She could see he was handsome, startlingly handsome. His hair was thick and wavy above dark brown eyes. His chin had a dimple.

Smiling at her warmly, Frederick Donovan held out a hymnal. "I would like to review the Sunday music. It will be my first service here, and I want to make a good impression. Do you have time?"

Nellie felt an immediate connection with the new preacher. She had not been in town long herself and had found it difficult to make friends with other young people. A few tried to include her, but she was a Yankee, after all.

"I'd be happy to," she smiled in return. "Why don't you sit next to me at the organ and we can decide the selections?"

Fred, as Nellie came to call him, was a popular addition to the little Florida church. He organized activities for the children and young people. He stopped into the Ladies' Guild meetings and complimented them on their work. The men found him affable and approachable. The senior pastor had only one criticism of Fred: his sermons were sometimes too full of "fire and brimstone."

"These are all good Christian people here, Fred," he'd admonish the younger man. "I'm not aware of any bank robbers, murderers or thieves in our congregation. You don't have to scare the daylights out of these folks."

Privately, Fred would complain to Nellie about the reprimands. "How can you expect people to be righteous if you don't put the fear of God into them?" he said in frustration. "I'm only trying to keep them in line, to guarantee their salvation. It's my duty." Nellie wasn't sure she agreed. She liked to think of God as a kind, forgiving, fatherly figure. Fred could get quite passionate when he started preaching—angry, in fact. Sometimes it frightened her.

However, Fred and Nellie worked closely in regard to the church's music. They chose the hymns and organ pieces together every week. Fred often came to choir practice and walked Nellie home afterward. She looked forward to every encounter.

After services one Sunday, Nellie stood in the church vestibule. Social-hour cookies and lemonade had been put out, and she sipped her drink slowly, keeping an eye out for Fred. Nellie knew that she was not the only female member of the congregation to find him engaging, so she took pains with her appearance every time she came to church.

Today, she wore a soft yellow dress with a wide sash of eyelet lace. It complimented her brown hair and brought out the blue in her eyes. At least that was what Fred had told her the last time she wore it. She had her favorite gold locket on, too. A few tendrils of hair, loosened from her Gibson girl pompadour, curled damply but charmingly down her neck. Even in September it was hot in Florida.

Suddenly, Nellie felt hands on her waist from behind and warm breath on the back on her neck.

"It's just me," Fred whispered.

A warm rush of pleasure ran through her along with a feeling of anxiety. She looked around quickly to see if anyone had observed this heady display of affection. Fred kept his hands on her and turned her around so she faced him, his arms now practically encircling her.

"Oh, Fred," Nellie said. "Not here in church!"

He only laughed. "Come outside. I need to speak to you."

Fred took Nellie's elbow and steered her outside. From there, they walked to a cluster of palm trees at the side of the church and stood in the shade. The sky was practically cloudless. A cow bird called from a bush. Parishioners began to leave, climbing into buggies and saying goodbye to friends and neighbors. No one seemed to take any notice of them.

Fred took Nellie's hands. "You won't believe what's happened," he told her, his face flushed with excitement. "I've been reassigned to Colorado!"

Nellie's heart sunk at the words. Fred was leaving for Colorado? It seemed as if he had only arrived. Besides, she had come to enjoy Fred's company immensely. Preparing the music with him was the bright spot in her week. She almost blushed as she thought of how her body tingled when he sat close to her on the organ bench, or when he reached across in front of her to point out a particular passage and brushed against her, steadying himself with his hand on her knee. She felt so dismayed at this news she almost did not hear what else he was saying.

"So, Nellie, what do you think? Will you move out to Colorado Springs with me and be my wife? A preacher's wife?"

Nellie thought her heart might stop. Tears filled her eyes so that she could barely see his face, looking at her with anticipation, waiting for an answer. She felt dizzy—so many thoughts suddenly filling her head!

The thoughts were not all happy, however. Nellie realized with a pang of dread that she had never discussed her health with Fred, or anyone in Florida. She had felt so much better here, stronger and with little cough. What would Fred think if she told him about the consumption now? What about the doctor's concerns if she became pregnant? Would Fred still want to marry her if she couldn't have children?

Nellie looked at Fred's hopeful, expectant face, and knew that being his wife would make her happier than she'd ever been. She dismissed all her fears.

"Oh, yes, Fred, yes, yes, yes!" She threw her arms around his neck wildly, hugging him close. He laughed and spun her around in the shade of the palms.

They were married in Deland a few weeks later before leaving for Colorado Springs. The congregation was delighted for the young couple and gave a picnic luncheon on the church lawn after the wedding ceremony. Despite her happiness, Nellie felt a bit homesick. Clifford was the only family member in attendance. How she wished her mother and aunts could have been there.

Colorado was very different from Florida and Michigan. The train trip from Fenton to Florida had gone through the Cumberland Mountains in Tennessee, but there was no comparison to the Rocky Mountains in Colorado. She loved how they rose up majestically into the clear blue sky, white caps of snow on top regardless of the season. Another thing that stood out was the vast expanses of land with no sign of houses or barns. The yellows and purples of the open range stretched out as far as the eye could see, with the occasional herd of cattle grazing or a bald eagle circling overhead. Even the air, so clear and dry, was different.

Fred and Nellie arrived in snowy, cold November. However, Nellie was surprised to find that it could be quite pleasant out-of-doors by midday, since the sun shone strongly most mornings. It was not at all like the biting, grey winter days in Michigan. She wore her bonnet outdoors faithfully, but her face and hands still browned from the sunshine.

Although the mountains towered in the distance, the town itself was very flat. Buildings and houses were few and far between with only scrubby little trees and small bushes struggling to survive in the hard ground. Most of the inhabitants didn't live in town. They were out on ranches, raising cattle or sheep. Nellie was surprised the first time she saw cowboys come into town. They wore big western hats—Fred told her they were called Stetson ten-gallon hats—and boots with spurs. Many of them carried rifles.

The frame parsonage the young couple lived in was rather plain, with none of the gingerbread trim Nellie was used to. Even so, she loved to sit in the rocker on the long low porch—unless the wind whipped up and blew dust everywhere.

Day after day, however, Nellie found herself exhausted after little exertion. There was no reason to worry, Fred told her, the high altitude was to blame. "The air is thinner up here. You'll get acclimated soon," he assured her.

Eventually, Nellie did begin to feel better—so healthy, in fact, that when she missed her monthly she did not give it much thought. As the next month rolled around and she began feeling queasy around food, Fred brought it up.

"Nellie, you've barely eaten today. Are you feeling all right?"

Fred looked carefully at his wife. He got up from the table, walked over, leaned down and kissed her softly on the top of her head.

"I don't know too much about this, but I'm wondering," he hesitated. "Do you think perhaps—?"

Nellie frowned. Slowly the realization hit her. After the doctor's warnings, she had just assumed that she could not—would not—get pregnant. *Oh, why worry?* she thought. She had been feeling so good out here! She was healthy again. Surely it would be all right.

After agreeing that Fred was probably correct, Nellie went to Dr. Garvin's office. It stood out among the more recently built store fronts, since it was the only single-pen log house chinked with clay. Nellie had walked past it many times. This time she paused, gathering her courage to go inside.

Fred worried about Nellie throughout her pregnancy. She seemed so delicate, unlike the hardy local women. Despite her previous fears, Nellie brushed off Fred's concerns. Excited about the baby, she sewed tiny gowns, shirts and bonnets. The church ladies made a beautiful baby quilt and presented it to her with pride. Fred commissioned a small wooden cradle from one of the parishioners. It was finished during Nellie's seventh month and sat, expectantly, in a corner of their bedroom.

Finally, it was time. When the pains began one morning, their intensity startled Nellie. It felt like someone was tightening a corset around her so tightly that she could not breathe. As the day wore on, the pains became stronger and closer together. Fred fetched Dr. Garvin.

The doctor hurried in to see Nellie and Fred was relegated to the front porch. Every scream from the bedroom tore through him. He paced nervously, then sat in Nellie's rocker, then paced again, wondering if every birth was like this.

Finally, a baby's thin wail pierced the night. Fred knocked on the bedroom door, anxious to see his wife and new baby.

"Just a few minutes," Dr. Garvin replied.

Fred gave the rocker a slight kick and paced some more.

At last Dr. Garvin came out of the bedroom, his shirtsleeves rolled up to his elbows. He looked rumpled and exhausted. "You can see your daughter," he said. "She's a beautiful little girl. Looks just like her mother."

The baby lay swaddled next to Nellie, who smiled up at Fred weakly, her face pale and tired. Fred held her hand. Even in the heat of the small bedroom, her hand felt cold. Nellie's eyes closed in exhaustion. Her breath was shallow. Fred looked at Dr. Garvin questioningly. The doctor nodded grimly towards the door.

"Doctor, how is Nellie? Is she alright?" Fred asked once they were in the hall.

The doctor hesitated. "Well, it is to be expected considering her condition."

Fred was confused. He remained silent, waiting for the doctor to explain.

"Surely you both knew the risk this pregnancy would be?" Dr. Garvin finally asked.

It was apparent from the look on Fred's face that he did not.

"I'm afraid we're just going to have to wait and see how she does," Dr. Garvin finished. "I'll come by tomorrow to check on them both."

Four days later Fred sent a telegram back to Nellie's family in Fenton.

*Baby girl born STOP Complications STOP Nellie is gone STOP Will bring baby by train. STOP*

Emma did not know how much more sorrow she could take. First her husband Judson and now her daughter Nellie— gone, so young, only twenty. Nellie hadn't even lived long enough to receive her father Judson's trust fund. Emma had so many regrets. She had been anxious to please her new husband, Hadley.

She had been busy with their own young daughter, Bessie. Now it was too late. Emma had missed her daughter Nellie's wedding, the birth of her first grandchild, and hadn't even had a chance to say goodbye. Now Fred was bringing the baby to Fenton. He had named the baby Nellie, after her mother. Perhaps he and little Nellie would stay in town and she could help raise the baby. It was her only consolation amidst the crushing sadness.

The November sky was overcast and the wind biting. Emma waited anxiously on the train platform, dressed in black mourning clothes. Julia, Win, Clifford and little Bessie stood with her. She was nervous to meet the stranger who had been Nellie's husband. *He's a widower now,* she told herself. *He is grieving as much as we are.* Finally, the train pulled into the station and stopped, small blasts of steam still coming from beneath the engine. The passengers began to disembark.

Fred was not hard to spot. Emma, however, didn't take in his features or demeanor when she saw him. She only had eyes for the small wrapped bundle in his arms.

The first few days were spent amiably. Everyone cooed and fussed over the baby. Gladly taking over the baby's care, Emma secured a wet nurse. She spent every available minute with little Nellie, even having the baby sleep in the master bedroom. Her new husband, Hadley, complained about his sleep being interrupted, but for once, Emma overruled him. She was busy but happy. Taking care of her granddaughter helped ease the pain of losing her daughter.

On the fourth day, Fred broached the issue of Nellie's trust fund.

"Oh, I'm afraid I don't know much about that," Emma told him. "Win and Julia handle all the money matters."

A meeting was set up with Win and Julia. Fred was shocked at what he heard. He turned away from Win's hard expression to face Emma.

"How do you expect me to raise your granddaughter on a clergyman's salary?" Fred asked in desperation. "This money was rightfully my wife's. We won't be cheated out of it just because she's gone!"

Emma gazed at the beautiful little baby in her arms and thought her heart would break. Little Nellie was so much like her mother! She turned and looked beseechingly at Julia. But Julia and Win were adamant.

"The trust Judson set up is quite simple," Win explained firmly. "Nellie was to inherit when she became of age at twenty-one. Now her daughter will inherit when she turns twenty-one. No sooner. The money will be kept safely for her until then."

"But surely Judson could not have anticipated these circumstances when he set up the trust," Emma pleaded. "Certainly he would want to provide for Nellie's daughter."

Win's expression did not change. "I'm sorry. The terms of the trust are quite clear."

Fred stared in disbelief at Julia and Win. His lips pressed together tightly, his face reddening with fury, he turned to Emma. Tears welled up in her eyes, but she did not speak.

"Well, then. You've left me no choice." Fred held his hands out for little Nellie. "I'm leaving. Give me the baby."

Emma instinctively held the baby closer. Where was Fred planning to go? Little Nellie had to stay in Fenton! She was Emma's only link to her oldest daughter!

"I said I'm leaving. I'll be taking little Nellie to my family in Indianapolis."

Choking back tears, Emma hugged the baby one last time. She wondered if Julia and Win understood the impact of their decision, of the fresh grief they were creating.

Fred took the baby from Emma's shaking arms.

"My family in Indianapolis will help raise her," he said bitterly. "Don't even think about contacting us. Consider yourselves cut out of her life!" Fred slammed the parlor door open and stormed out.

# 9
# *Fenton High School Class '04*

### 1900—1904

Fenton High School. Photo courtesy of A J Phillips Historical Museum

In the fall of 1900, Clifford joined the freshman class at Fenton High School. He had been absent from town for several years since the death of his father. First he was at the military school in Orchard Lake and then in Florida with Nellie. However, he remembered most of his classmates from years before at South Ward School. They had spent many hours playing games in the schoolyard, swimming in the Shiawassee River below Whittle's Brewing and fishing in the Fenton Mill Pond. Reunited with his old pals, it did not take long for Clifford to fit in as if he had never been away.

Clifford played first base on the baseball team. That first year saw games against the high school teams in Flint, Howell, Linden and Clarkston. Sophomore year, Lansing and Detroit Central High School were added to the schedule and Fenton emerged state champion. During his senior year, Clifford was elected captain of the team.

After losing their coach, football hadn't been played in Fenton for several years. It started up again during Clifford's junior year with good results, but no one thought to organize a team for the following year. A new teacher, Mr. Chapman, had played football at State Normal. He volunteered to coach if a team was organized. Since it was already late September, everyone had to scramble. Will Clements was elected captain. Clifford played fullback and was team manager. Practice began in earnest right away—two hours daily of drills, scrimmage and running. The uniforms—dirty, worn-out moleskins which had served many a boy over the years—were kept down in the boiler room.

Since the season was already well under way, only two games were scheduled. The first was on November 7th, against Howell High School. The Fenton team started strong, scoring three touchdowns.

The Fenton girls, all wearing little hats perched on their heads, cheered the boys on through their megaphones: "Boom-a-likker, boom-a-likker, sis boom bah! Fenton High School! Rah! Rah! Rah!"

In the second half, Howell scored a touchdown. They claimed another when a punted ball bounced over the Howell goal line and was seized by one of their players. But when time was called, Fenton had the ball, rushing it steadily into Howell territory and past the goal line. Victory!

The return game

Fenton High School Football Team—1903.
Clifford Phillips upper right corner

was played in Howell on November 14th. It was summed up nicely in the Fentonian yearbook:

*"The horse-drawn bus that carried the Fenton team to Howell was five and a half hours on the road and long after noon unloaded a tired lot at the hotel door. Owing to their worn condition, the boys expected to be beaten, and the game more than justified their fears. The Fenton players were stiff and tired, and they found that the Howell referee, backed by the crowd, cheated them at every opportunity. They gave up hope of winning, tho' they played gamely to the last. Considerable difficulty was encountered in driving home, probably due to darkness and the disheartened condition of the players. One or two seemed indifferent to defeat, but the majority were visibly affected by their misfortune. While it cannot be said that the team of '03 ended its short season in a blaze of glory, yet it can safely be said that had it been earlier, it would, in all probability, have astonished the town."*

And so the season ended one and one.

# 10
## SS Arabic

### 1904

Clifford leaned out the open train window to wave at his fiancé Mabel, his mother Emma and his little half-sister Bessie, who were standing on the platform. Bessie hid her face in Emma's skirts and then peeked out at her big brother, tears blurring her vision. Mabel dabbed at her face with her handkerchief but waved at Clifford bravely. The conductor hollered, "All aboard!" and swung up on the caboose. The steam whistle shrieked as the train started chugging—slowly at first, then gradually gaining momentum.

Clifford watched as the figures of his family grew smaller and smaller. He sighed and sat back in the comfortable Pullman berth. His new book, "The Call of the Wild," lay unopened on the seat beside him. Reaching into his jacket pocket, Clifford pulled out the small blue ring box his mother had given to him the night before.

She had knocked on his bedroom door and came in as he finished packing his steamer trunk.

"I've been waiting for the right time to give this to you," she said. "My father gave it to me before I married your father and it served us well." She held her hand out with the box.

Mystified, Clifford took it from her. He lifted the top and saw a delicate ring of gold and silver intertwined bands laying on the white satin. He looked up at his mother questioningly. It was much too feminine for a man to wear.

"Is this for me to give to Mabel?" he asked.

"No. It's called a lover's knot. My father gave it to me before your father and I started courting. He explained that marriage was more than just romance and fantasy. The person you choose to be your spouse will determine the rest of your life, your home, your children. When you think about your future and who you want to share it with, think of this ring The gold and the silver are each separate, yet intertwined to make a beautiful whole. Ask yourself, will this person complete your lover's knot?"

Clifford nodded but he was a little confused. His mother knew he and Mabel planned to marry next year. His mind was on the upcoming trip tomorrow so he shoved the box in his pocket and kissed his mother on the cheek. Now he settled back in the train seat and examined the ring more closely. He and Mabel were engaged, and he was sure she was the one. He didn't need a ring to tell him. Strange that his mother felt this was a good time to give it to him. Well, it would be a good reminder to do everything he could to make Mabel happy—to try and be the kind of man she would want to complete her knot.

Clifford carefully replaced the ring in the box and looked across the compartment at Allan Gunning, his traveling companion. Many people in town considered Allan eccentric. Tall and husky, he wore his beard unfashionably long and full. A close family friend he was twenty years older than Clifford and still a bachelor. Allan was headed back to England to visit his family. It had been Aunt Julia's graduation gift to Clifford to travel with him. While it was not the grand tour many wealthy young men took after finishing high school, it was a chance for Clifford to see something of the world before he settled down. His mother, Emma, was unsure of the plan at first, but finally acquiesced to Julia's wishes, as she usually did. Clifford's sweetheart, Mabel, was also unhappy about him leaving. He assured her he would return in plenty of time to be married next June, as they planned.

Although it was never talked about, having a stepfather had been difficult for Clifford. Memories of his father were still fresh and no one could take his place. He missed his sister Nellie, too. Now with a stepfather, a younger half-sister in the family and another baby on the way, Clifford sometimes felt like an outsider in his own family. He was glad to get away for a while.

In Detroit, they switched trains for the final leg of the trip to New York. The passenger car of this train was roomier, with tufted bench seats and high arched ceilings. After they settled in, Clifford peppered Allan with questions about England, but Allan soon dozed off. Clifford picked up his book, but was too restless to read.

The conductor, strolling by, noticed the young man staring out the window. "You know, there's an observation car if you care to have a better view," he told Clifford.

Eagerly, Clifford rose and followed him to the end of the car. The conductor slid the door open, and a burst of air struck them as he stepped out onto the small walkway connecting the two rail cars. The platform jumped and jerked precariously. Grabbing a railing to steady himself, Clifford nervously looked down at the couplings holding the two cars together, with the railroad tracks racing below them. His heart quickened, he took a deep breath, and stepped down too.

The conductor didn't miss a stride. In two confident steps, he reached the door to the next car and slid it open. Clifford hesitated for a moment, then grabbed another railing tightly as he stepped between the swaying cars. He was relieved to land on the solid floor of the observation car.

The conductor, smiling, motioned to a plush swivel armchair. Clifford gratefully sat down in front of the glass windows and domed ceiling. He spent the next few hours watching the farm lands and small villages of Ohio fly by.

Dinner was served in a well-appointed dining car, with linen, china and silver comparable to that of a fine hotel. They ate roast beef and gravy with new potatoes and peas. Chocolate cake and coffee was offered for dessert.

By the time Clifford and Allan returned to their compartment, the train was racing through Pennsylvania in the dark. The flames from the gas chandeliers flickered overhead with the swaying of the cars. The sleeping berths had been made up, and the two settled in for the night. Clifford tried to hide his amusement at Allan's difficulty in folding his long legs into the short bed.

The next morning, they awoke in New York City. As the porters unloaded their trunks from the train, Allan signaled for a two-wheel hansom cab. The driver was a burly man, his skin reddish and rough, a flannel flat cap on his head. His dappled gray mare hung her head, patiently waiting. She whinnied and snorted when Clifford patted her soft nose.

Sinewy forearms bulging under a worn cotton work shirt, the driver swung the heavy trunks up on the cab. Despite clutching a pipe in his teeth, he managed to spit out two words, in a thick Irish brogue. "Where to?"

"The harbor," Allan answered. "SS Arabic."

After a grunt and a nod from the driver, who introduced himself as Seamus, they climbed into the open cab. Seamus hoisted himself onto the front bench seat. Clifford and Allan took seats behind him.

Seamus pocketed his pipe and took the reins, "Ye heard 'bout the horrible accident at the harbor, coupla weeks ago?" he asked. "Terrable."

Clifford and Allan certainly had heard. It had been in all the newspapers. An old side-wheel steamboat, the SS General Slocum, had caught fire and sank as it was ferrying over 1,300 passengers to a church picnic. Most of them had been lost. It was sobering to think of that recent tragedy as they headed to the harbor.

"Nodda worry," Seamus continued, as if he had read their minds. "The SS Arabic just launched lass year. She's a fine, sturdy ship, she is. Steel hulled."

His passengers nodded and smiled, but not convincingly enough for Seamus.

"Buck up, boys. Ye be fine," he grinned. Seamus gave a soft flick of his whip and a click-click of his tongue. The mare lifted her head and plodded into traffic, her hoofs clopping on the brick pavement.

Clifford looked around at the city as they moved along. New York seemed similar to Detroit, only much bigger. Both cities had skyscrapers stretching up into the clouds. At street level, the roads were crowded with horse-drawn street cars and hurrying people. Construction was everywhere.

"What's that?" Clifford asked, pointing to a small area of heavy iron fencing jutting out of the sidewalk.

"Called the subway," Seamus answered. "Stairs going unnerground to trains running through tunnels. Supposed to be working this fall. Who woulda thought?"

He chuckled and shook his head. "I jess hope it donna put me and me mare outta business. First the new electric carriages and now this subway. No, I donna think anything will ever replace the horse."

As they approached the harbor, a cool breeze began to blow and Clifford could actually taste the salt in the air. The cab turned and clattered onto the wooden wharf. The SS Arabic loomed ahead, moored at the pier. Her black hull stretched over 600 feet in length, and her single smokestack—beige with a wide black smoke band—rose up in the center. There were two masts in the front and two in the back. The British Union Jack flew on the first mast and the red White Star banner on the second. Four more decks rose above the main deck. An island bridge house sat far forward with two other short blocks aft.

Seamus drove past a gangplank that led down to the cargo hold. "They be loading cargo here for the trip over," he explained, pointing. "Coming back, she'll be bringing immigrants, mostly from me country, Ireland. I'm here two years now, she's a great country, she is. Been saving up for me sweetheart to come."

Seamus expertly maneuvered the cab further down the wharf, weaving around the longshoremen and baggage wagons, until he stopped at the main gangplank. "This be where ye board," he said. Clifford and Allan climbed down. Allan paid Seamus, who nodded in appreciation. "Thankee. Ahl make sure ye luggage gets loaded on. Are ye first or second class?"

"Second," replied Allan.

"Smart choice," the driver said. "Almost as fancified as first class, but easier on the wallet." He chuckled. "Not that I've seen it myself, a'course."

With a gentle flick of Seamus' whip, the mare picked up her head and began to walk. "Have a safe voyage, fellers!" he called as the cab moved away.

Clifford and Allan joined the other passengers heading up the gangplank. On deck stood the captain and his staff to greet them. The captain was a tall man with a neatly trimmed beard, he had an air of confident authority. His white linen single-breasted uniform, with a stiff Russian collar and five brass buttons down the front, was crisply starched. Several medals were pinned proudly above his left breast. His shoulder boards were black with four bands of gold piping. A white peaked hat with the White Star emblem surrounded by gold leaves on the bill sat atop his graying hair.

"Welcome aboard!" The captain shook Clifford's hand, then Allan's. He gestured to a row of uniformed men. "One of the stewards will show you to your cabin. Your trunks will be delivered to you before supper. We're set to depart tomorrow morning bright and early."

Clifford and Allan followed the steward down two flights of stairs and along a narrow corridor. Their cabin looked quite comfortable—two separate berths one atop the other, a washbowl, and a built-in settee. Allan stretched out on the lower berth and settled back with his hands clasped behind his head. "I'm just going to catch a little shut eye," he said, yawning.

Clifford shook his head at Allan's nonchalance. He felt too excited to be cooped up in the small cabin and decided to explore. At the ship's center, he found a wide, curved stairway, elaborately decorated with thick red and white patterned carpet runners and intricate brass balustrades. Climbing several flights, Clifford found himself on the uppermost forward deck, just outside the dining salon, which was the full width of the ship.

The salon walls were polished mahogany. The ceiling was a two-story glass dome. Sunlight sparkled off flower-filled crystal vases and the china and silver the stewards were setting out for tea. Clifford noticed that the round tables and swivel chairs were fixed to the floor.

Continuing to explore, Clifford then discovered the library. The ceiling and frieze were all in a lustrous cream and gold lincrusta. The walls of the library were paneled in a light polished oak with handsome carvings, nicely setting off the parquet floor. The room was filled with comfortable couches, leather chairs and Chippendale writing tables. Heavy velvet draperies hung on the large windows and potted ferns were scattered throughout.

Other areas of the ship held a smoking room, a large ballroom, a two-chair barber shop and a gift shop. Never had Clifford seen so much grandeur!

After exploring for close to an hour, he stopped on the promenade deck to take in the view of the ships in the harbor and the New York skyline. The sun sparkled on the choppy water and he could hear a ship horn in the distance as he leaned against the railing, grasping the polished wood.

"Have you found everything you need, Sir?"

Clifford turned to the uniformed purser standing next to him.

"Yes, thank you," he said. "I'm just finding my way around. It's my first time sailing."

"She's certainly a fine ship," the purser stated proudly. "Over 16,000 tons with twin screws. Our top speed is 16 knots—we'll make the passage in nine days!"

Clifford nodded as if he understood the technical terms. "She's a beauty!" he agreed.

The purser cleared his throat. His next words were polite and hesitant. "But sir, once we're underway, you'll be required to stay on the second-class decks. This here's first class."

Chagrined, Clifford moved away from the railing as the steward hurried away. Suddenly, he heard a soft giggle. Sitting in a rattan deck chair behind him was a young woman who looked to be about Mabel's age. He hadn't noticed her there. She wore a green ruffled dress and held a matching lace-trimmed parasol in gloved hands. Thick copper-colored curls tumbled past her milky white neck and her feet were tucked demurely under the chair.

"Forgive me," she said. "I shouldn't have laughed."

Gathering her skirt, she rose from her seat and walked over to Clifford.

"I'm Penelope Maitland." She smiled demurely, extending her hand. "And your name?"

He was momentarily tongue-tied. "Clifford," he finally said. "Clifford Phillips."

"Hello, Clifford. It's certainly nice to meet someone my age. We're going to be stuck on this floating hotel for at least eight days. It's usually so incredibly boring." She turned towards the railing and looked out.

"Oh, it's not boring to me," Clifford replied. "This is my first time going abroad. I've never seen anything quite like this."

"Really?" she said coquettishly. "I never would have guessed. You look to be a man of the world. I bet you're a good dancer."

Clifford felt flattered, but he had to be honest. "I'm glad to meet you, too, but I don't think we'll be seeing each other much, Miss Maitland. As you heard, we're second class, and I'm guessing you're not."

"We?" She arched her eyebrow.

"I'm traveling with a family friend. He's going back to see his family in England and I'm lucky enough to be accompanying him."

"I see." Penelope sighed. "I'm afraid I've made this voyage more than once. It gets old. When Papa has business in London, Mama and I go on to Worth's in Paris to order our wardrobe for the season." She paused and then added, "Some trips are worse than others. The weather can be bad and the seas rough. Then it's not much fun at all. Luckily, I don't get seasick, but Mama does. She can be absolutely miserable."

Penelope turned, twirling her parasol. "Speaking of Mama, she'll wonder where I've wandered off to. I'd better get back before she starts looking for me." She held her gloved hand out, and Clifford shook it.

Penelope giggled, "Now don't let the whole first class thing be a deterrent, Clifford. You can always be my guest. You see, Mama usually picks out one or two of the young men on board who she deems appropriate suitors." Penelope sighed impishly and twisted a ringlet with her gloved finger. "Then I have to spend the entire voyage fighting them off." She wrinkled her nose and giggled again before turning away. "I'm counting on you to be my knight in shining armor and help discourage them."

Clifford watched her depart, skirt swaying and red curls dancing along her back. She stopped, turned and looked at him and then continued on. He was not at all sure what to think of Miss Penelope Maitland.

It was time for supper when Clifford returned to his cabin, and he and Allan quickly found their way to the second class dining room. It was not very different from the first class dining room. The tables were long and rectangular instead of round, but they were still covered in white linen tablecloths, topped with glass flower vases, and bolted to the floor. Menus, printed on postcards, sat in a small silver stand at each place setting. Under the heading "White Star Line" was a drawing of the ship with an American flag and a Union Jack in the corners. It would be a nice souvenir to send to Mabel. The blue floral-edged china was decorated with the flag of the White Star Line: a red split-tail flag with a white star. The flag was also etched on the handles of all the silverware. In fact, everything Clifford could see seemed to be emblazoned with the ship's name and the flag of the White Star Line.

The ship's departure began the next morning, with much fanfare. Clifford found a spot at the main deck's crowded railing to watch. The orchestra sat in a semi-circle on deck and played while the crowds down on the pier threw streamers and confetti and waved handkerchiefs.

After two large blasts from the ship's horn, they began to move. Clifford saw a small tugboat pushing the SS Arabic away from her berth and out into the harbor. The early morning sun beat down on Clifford's shoulders as he watched the shoreline of New York City slip by. A shiver of excitement ran though him as Lady Liberty came into view. She had been a gift from France only thirty years prior. He had read about the installation of the statue in the harbor, and seeing her in person made him feel a pang of patriotism and wonder. She was perched atop a stone pedestal; her weathered surfaces shone green in the early sunlight. A spiked crown on her head, the massive statue held a book in her left hand and a torch in her raised right hand. Clifford couldn't take his eyes off her until Allan strolled up next to him.

"The Statue of Liberty. First sight I had when we reached America," Allan said. They both stared as the ship slid past the statue. Soon, another small island with several large buildings came into view.

"That's Ellis Island," Allan remarked. "I remember that, too, but not as fondly. All us immigrants were taken off the ship there. Everyone had to be examined by a doctor before we could enter the country. The people who weren't healthy had to return to the ship. Sometimes the process took several days. It was a worry to come all that way and then wonder if you'd be sent back."

Clifford stayed on deck after Allan and most of the other passengers dispersed. He watched the shoreline disappear until all he could see was the Atlantic. It was a relatively calm day, with a warm sun and soft sea breeze. The boat vibrated slightly from the churning of the powerful engines and there was the pungent smell of fuel in the air. Clifford wandered the deck for an hour, politely greeting other passengers who sat reading or smoking.

That afternoon at tea, a steward approached their table, carrying a note on a silver tray. "Mr. Phillips?" he inquired. Clifford nodded and the steward handed him the note. Puzzled, the young man unfolded it and read. *Meet me outside the first class dining room after supper.* It was signed *P.M.*

"What's that?" Allan asked.

Clifford didn't meet Allan's curious gaze. "An acquaintance I met on deck yesterday."

Allan's expression turned into a bemused frown.

"Actually, it was a young lady," admitted Clifford. "She wants me to meet her after supper."

Allan chuckled, "Watch yourself. Shipboard romance is a nice diversion, but remember—that's all it is."

"No need to worry about that," Clifford quickly replied. "For one thing, I have Mabel. For another, this young lady is traveling first class." And for an instant, the image of his mother's ring box and the lover's knot ring came to mind.

"Whatever you say," said Allan agreeably, but he gave a knowing grin.

After supper, Clifford cautiously made his way up to the first-class deck. Maybe he'd do all right. As far as he could tell, there was not much difference between first class and second class accommodations, except for the fact that in second class he didn't have to worry about bumping into a Vanderbilt or a Rockefeller—or Penelope's mother.

He stood outside the double doors to the dining room, staying in the shadows. After a few minutes, the handsomely dressed diners began to come out, chatting gaily. Clifford spotted Penelope with her parents. She wore a soft yellow gown, the flimsy fabric floating in the night breeze. He noticed all the gentlemen in first class were in formal evening dress. He was wearing the same suit he had worn all day. Hit with a moment of panic, Clifford wondered how soon he would be found out and ordered to leave the deck.

Penelope caught his eye, but ignored him and continued walking. Then she spoke. "Mama, Papa, I think I'll take a stroll out on the deck. It's such a beautiful night. I won't be long." She watched her parents depart. When they were out of sight, she turned and flounced back to Clifford.

"You can come out of the shadows now," Penelope laughed. "Let's walk." She took his elbow and steered him away to a darker, less populated area of the deck.

"I love it out here," Penelope whispered, leaning on the railing. The sky and sea were both black as pitch, accentuating the moonlight dancing on the crest of the waves and the stars dotting the sky overhead. She turned to smile at Clifford. "Don't you adore the stars? I wish I knew more about them. Do you know the night sky?"

"Actually, I—I do," Clifford answered nervously, glad for his military school training in navigation by the stars.

"Really? How marvelous!" Penelope put a white, delicate hand on Clifford's arm. "Well, tell me about the stars, then!"

Clifford took a deep breath and began to talk. He proceeded to point out the constellations: the North Star, the Big Dipper and the Little Dipper. For the first time since he had met Penelope, he began to feel comfortable.

"Look at that," he said, pointing. "It's so dark out here you can even see Draco, the Dragon."

Suddenly afraid that he was boring her, Clifford glanced down at Penelope. To his relief, she gazed up at him with a warm smile.

"There's a ball after supper tomorrow night," she said. "Can you get away? Mama has already found several prospects for me and I need your help keeping them at bay." She laughed and touched his arm again. "You can be my mysterious gentleman suitor."

Clifford hesitated. He had never met a girl quite like Penelope. Her red curls were piled on top of her head, showing off small diamond teardrop earrings that glistened in the moonlight. Her gown was cut low and a delicate gold filigree locket rested on her décolletage.

He turned away and looked out at the calm sea. The ship powered along smoothly, in contrast to his churning thoughts. The nearness of this charming and beautiful girl—the excitement of the new and unknown—all mixed up with images of home and Mabel.

*Oh, don't be such a rube,* Clifford scolded himself, shaking his head to clear it. *She's just a nice girl that needs help.*

He turned to look at Penelope and returned her smile. "How can I refuse?"

# 11
## China Painting

1904

Left to right: Cora Peer, Myrtle Vilert, Georgia Zellner, Mabel Corrigan

Now that they had graduated from high school, Mabel missed seeing her friends every day. She was usually the one to organize their get-togethers and her mother suggested she plan a china painting party, which was all the rage.

Mabel visited Mrs. Beadle's china shop to assemble the supplies—blank plates, brushes and paint. Mabel decided on a pattern with purple violets and several large green leaves. Mrs. Beadle gave her a few tips on getting the shading just right, and she had practiced with the brushes and paints on heavy paper before the girls arrived. It wasn't easy.

Of course, she invited her best friends: Myrtle Vilert, Cora Peer, and Georgia Zellner.

The quote under Mabel's picture in the yearbook was "A rose bud set with little willful thorns." She may have been strong-willed, but Mabel was quick to laugh and was kind to everyone. She had a round, pretty face, with a slight space between her two front teeth. Her dark brown hair was piled up in a very fashionable pompadour.

The party took place on a warm summer day. The bay windows in the dining room had been opened, lace curtains billowing ever so slightly in the breeze. The large elm tree in the side yard kept the house cool even in the summer heat.

The girls sat around the Corrigan's dining room table, discussing their future plans and reminiscing about school. Even though most of them had elected the arduous Latin course of study, high school had still been a whirlwind of fun.

I just can't believe it's all behind us," said Cora, picking up a small lemon biscuit and taking a nibble. "What's to become of us? Marriage? Broods of children?" They laughed at the thought.

"Do you remember that first winter of high school?" Myrtle asked. "There was so much snow. We were able to sled for days."

The newspapers had called it the Great Blizzard of 1899. Snow fell as far south as Tallahassee, Florida, and frost was reported in Cuba.

"How about riding through town after the first sledding party?" recalled Georgia. "We had a talking-to the next morning because the neighbors complained about the racket so late at night!"

"That's when we first got to know Clifford," Cora giggled. "We all thought he was a dreamboat!" She glanced slyly toward Mabel, who had been intently painting the gold edging on her plate.

Mabel looked up. "You just keep your mind on your own beau, now, Cora!" she scolded, only half joking.

Myrtle continued reminiscing, "My favorite was Georgia's party during sophomore year. Remember the souvenirs with gilded writing proclaiming 'Class of '04.' It was so exciting to see. I think that's the first time I actually thought about graduation. It seemed such a long way off then. Look at us now!"

The girls sighed, and turned back to painting their plates.

Mabel paused, brush suspended in air, remembering. "I think my favorite memory was when we performed *The Cool Collegians* at the Junior Exhibition." She had played the main character and Clifford was the male lead in the play. What a grand time they had, learning their lines together and practicing.

"Well, I'm sure it would be," said Cora. "That's when it became obvious to the rest of us that you were Clifford's girl." Mabel blushed and smiled. Cora continued, "My favorite memory was when we held a reception for the Senior Class of 1903. I think that was the best party ever. Remember the large banner over the entrance and the Japanese lanterns strung around the veranda. I've never been to anything so elegant."

"I think you're right," chimed in Georgia. "With the mandolin and guitar music, it was grand."

"Hey, what about the Halloween party Mable gave senior year?" Myrtle interjected. "Your invitations were so cute! Kum ter our hous Hollow'een Nite. Oh, and you sealed them with a skull and crossbones and dancing skeletons. Now that was a party to remember!"

"Mabel, your plate is turning out so well. Show us how you are doing that edging," said Cora. "My goodness, it's as good as Mrs. Beadle's. Oh, I hope I get one of her plates for my hope chest."

"I can't believe we are the last class out of Fenton High School," said Georgia.

"The last class?" asked Cora, puzzled.

"Well, the last class out of old Fenton High, anyway," Georgia explained, "The school is going to be remodeled this summer. How sad. We had so many good times there. I wonder if it will even seem like our school anymore."

"Cheer up," said Mabel. "I'm glad Clifford had the idea to take one of the glass transom windows that was being removed and etch it with all our names. The Class of '04 will be remembered forever."

"That's not all our class will be remembered for!" laughed Cora. "Senior Prank—when the boys rolled the Civil War cannon from the Water Works Park up to the front of the school. Miss Woods was not happy about that. No one ever owned up to it, but I think it was another one of Clifford's ideas. "

Mable kept her head down, concentrating on her work, trying not to laugh. Cora was right about one thing. Mable was definitely Clifford's girl. Before he left for England, they had been officially betrothed. However, despite Clifford's promise that he would be back to settle down with her in Fenton, Mabel had a small niggling fear. Would he still feel that way after seeing New York City and London?

Mabel thought wistfully of the cedar hope chest upstairs in her bedroom. The Van Atta Furniture Company had given one to all the girls in the Class of '04 as a graduation gift. Mabel and her friends often exchanged teacups and saucers or monogrammed silver pieces for birthdays and special occasions. Those items were quickly stored in their new chests.

Mabel planned to really fill hers up this summer while Clifford was gone. If her painted plate turned out, she would add it as well. She carefully turned the plate over, signed her name and dated it.

"So Mabel, have you heard from Clifford?"

# 12

## *Travel Abroad*

1904

---

The next morning in the harsh light of day, Clifford began to have second thoughts about keeping the promise he had made to Penelope. Things were getting complicated. Sneaking up to the first-class deck was not the only obstacle. He also had to find an appropriate evening suit.

After breakfast, Clifford wandered to the second-class deck and began to pace nervously, wondering what to do. He greeted an older couple who were sitting on wicker deck chairs, wrapped in woolen blankets to protect them from the chilly morning air. A young purser had just cleared the couple's coffee service. He glanced up at Clifford, nodded in recognition and walked over. It was the same purser Clifford had spoken to the first day on board.

"And you, sir? Is there anything I can get for you?" the purser asked as he approached. As he got closer to Clifford, he grinned and leaned in. "Staying out of first class now, are you?" he asked slyly.

Clifford's blush answered the question.

"I see," nodded the purser. "I thought I might have seen you last night on the first-class deck, talking with Miss Penelope. But then I told myself I must have been mistaken. Perhaps it was someone who looked like you."

To Clifford's relief, the purser seemed to be amused by last night's transgression. His friendly smile showed a hint of camaraderie. Clifford leaned in, too. "I'm afraid I've got myself in a pickle," he admitted in a whisper.

The purser raised his eyebrows. "Knowing Miss Penelope Maitland, I'm not surprised." He nodded sympathetically. "And I doubt you'll be the last young man so affected. What's the problem?"

"I'm to meet her at the ball tonight."

"Well, sneaking up to first class shouldn't be difficult," the purser whispered back. "You've done it before."

"But I don't have evening dress," Clifford explained. "I'll stand out like a sore thumb."

"Ah. That is a problem." The purser contemplated the tray in his hands and took a minute to move the empty china cups around, thinking. Then, he stepped back and looked Clifford up and down. "Let me check the laundry," he said. "There just might be a suit about your size, waiting to be delivered. I hope I don't take it to the wrong cabin by mistake. I tend to be careless sometimes." The purser winked as he hefted the tray to his shoulder and turned to leave. "Have a nice day, sir."

That afternoon, the evening suit appeared in their cabin. "So you're going to dress the part tonight?" asked Allan.

"Penelope asked a favor of me, that's all," Clifford answered.

Allan shook his head, but made no further comment.

At supper, the steward held the upholstered swivel chairs for Clifford and Allan. It still seemed odd to sit at tables and chairs that were bolted to the floor. Clifford fiddled with his napkin while Allan picked up the menu from the silver place holder. "You should send this home," Allan said. "To your mother, or Mabel."

The mention of Mabel's name did nothing to calm Clifford's discomfort. In fact, it made his nervousness worse.

Allan smirked. "Quite a selection of dishes, as always," he remarked, glancing over the menu. "Not hungry, Clifford? Fillet of brill or egg L'Argenteuil doesn't appeal to you? Perhaps salmon mayonnaise, potted shrimps, or veal and ham pie?"

Clifford gave his friend a rueful look and sipped his water. How had he gotten himself into this mess?

"I'm probably just a little seasick," he said.

Allan leaned in. "Is it seasickness or your conscience?" he asked.

Clifford knew the answer to that, but he was stuck. He had given Penelope his word. Allan grew tired of teasing Clifford, and the rest of the meal passed in near silence.

After supper, Clifford hurried back to the cabin to change clothes. He pulled on the dark high-waisted trousers and the dress shirt, the starched front of which was decorated with studs. Over that, he fastened the white waistcoat and tied the white bow tie over the winged shirt collar. The purser had done a good job of guessing his size.

Allan sat on the settee and shook his head. "You look pretty good," he admitted, "but what about your shirt sleeves? I don't know who loaned you this suit, but he forgot the cufflinks."

Clifford looked down at the open cuffs. "Oh, no," he sighed. "What do I do?"

"Don't worry. I have a pair." Allan jumped up and reached for a small drawer in his open steamer trunk. "Luckily, they're mother-of-pearl and will match the shirt studs."

"Thanks," said Clifford gratefully, quickly fastening the cuffs. Lastly, he pulled on the evening coat with its shawl collar, silk facings and a single button. The pants were a little long, but he hoped they would camouflage his everyday lace-up oxford shoes. He certainly didn't own a pair of the appropriate opera pumps.

"Not bad," nodded Allan.

Clifford stood back and admired himself in the small mirror over the sink. The year at military school had left him with excellent posture, and he cut a dashing figure, he had to admit. If Mabel could see him now.

Mabel! The thought of his sweetheart took the smile off Clifford's face. What would she think about him sneaking into first class for a rendezvous with another girl? She wouldn't be happy, he was sure of that. But Penelope was persuasive, and he was only trying to help her out. Still, it would be hard to explain to anyone back home.

Pushing thoughts of Mabel from his mind, Clifford left the cabin and made his way to the first-class deck. He followed the sound of the orchestra to the grand ballroom, waited until a large group of passengers entered and followed them in. A sudden fear froze him in his tracks—what if the owner of this fine suit recognized it on him.

*That's silly,* he said to himself. *All these snooty suits look alike.*

Clifford took a deep breath and looked around. The room was magnificent, with rainbows of light sparkling from the crystals of the ornate electrified chandeliers. The ballroom was awash with color—women in lavish ball gowns, jewels and tiaras floating among lush flower arrangements on the walls and tables. The men, all in white tie, gracefully led their partners around the parquet floor. Those not dancing stood in small groups, engaged in earnest conversation.

Nervously, Clifford looked around for Penelope. After a few moments, he spotted her in the middle of a cluster of young men. Nodding politely, but looking a little bored, she broke into a grin when she saw Clifford.

Emboldened, he walked over. Penelope did not bother to introduce him to the others, but tilted her head and offered him her hand. Clifford paused briefly, then kissed her hand gallantly, not sure if this was the correct thing to do. Life in first class was very different from dances in Fenton.

"You'll have to excuse us," Penelope said to her surprised entourage, "but I've promised Mr. Phillips this dance." Clifford could feel their cold glares as he and

Penelope walked on to the dance floor.

The orchestra was playing a waltz. Clifford held Penelope's right arm out to the side and with his other arm encircled her waist. She rested her left hand on his arm. He gave a quick thanks to Aunt Julia for her insistence on dance lessons, and they slid in among the other dancers.

"Thank goodness you made it!" Penelope whispered. "I thought I would die of boredom." She glanced behind Clifford. "Oh, Mama is watching. She will want to know who you are. What story shall we come up with? A duke? A land baron?" She giggled. "Do you think you could affect a foreign accent?"

Clifford smiled. In spite of his nerves, being with Penelope was exciting and fun. "I probably look too young to be a duke or baron. It's hard enough playing at being a proper gentleman—wouldn't that suit you?"

She threw her head back and laughed, "Proper? Oh, no! Not you, too! I've had my fill of proper gentlemen."

As the waltz ended, Clifford steered Penelope across the room from her admirers. A waiter approached with a tray of champagne flutes. Clifford and Penelope each took a glass. She raised hers in a mock toast, "To the mysterious Count Philippe! My hero!"

As they drank the cold, sparkly beverage, Clifford noticed one of the neglected suitors. Tall and gangly, he marched deliberately through the throng of dancers towards them. Moving swiftly, Clifford took Penelope's glass and set it with his own on the nearest table. He took her hand, moved to the center of the floor, and started dancing to the lively two-step the orchestra had begun playing. At the end of the song, they stopped to catch their breath. Clifford looked around for any other suitors to appear, ready to whirl Penelope into a fox-trot, a waltz, or even a tango in order to keep her away from the wolves.

The two continued to dance for several more numbers, enduring the stares of Penelope's would-be partners. The rejected suitors watched helplessly as the couple glided around the floor, Clifford holding the laughing Penelope protectively close. This game of cat and mouse might have lasted all night, had it not been for Penelope's father, who strode up to Clifford and Penelope as soon as the orchestra took a break.

Penelope's father was not a large gentleman, but he had the air of someone used to getting his way. Hair parted in the middle and slicked back, a dark mustache carefully waxed to turn up at the ends, his evening suit was as impeccable as his grooming.

"Penelope, my dear—" he began as he approached his daughter.

Penelope turned and feigned surprise. "Oh, Papa! Why, where have you been?"

Mr. Maitland didn't respond, but eyed his daughter's dancing partner suspiciously. He held his hands clasped behind his back and did not extend a hand to shake Clifford's.

"Penelope, who is this young man? I don't believe I've seen him in the dining room."

Penelope turned back to Clifford. "Father, may I present Mr. Clifford Phillips."

"Phillips, eh? I'm not familiar with your family. Are you from New York?"

"No, sir." Clifford looked anxiously at Penelope, who shrugged and smiled, then back at her father. "Um—Michigan."

"Michigan!" The word seemed to leave a bad taste in his mouth. "Good heavens! That's practically the Wild West. What is your family's business there?"

"Oh, father, please!" Penelope cried. "Does everything have to be about business? Clifford and I are just having a little fun." She clung to Clifford's arm and pouted prettily.

"We're in manufacturing, sir," Clifford put in hurriedly. "A.J. Phillips & Co."

"Never heard of it," Mr. Maitland harrumphed. He then turned his attention to his daughter. "I'm sure this young man is a decent chap, my dear, but life is not all fun and games. You need to mingle."

Penelope pouted again, looking for all the world like a naughty little girl about to stamp her foot and have a tantrum.

Her father gave her a warning look. She dropped Clifford's arm. He went on.

"Your mother's gone to a lot of trouble to be sure you were introduced to the suitable young men on board. You must dance with them, too. You can't let one person monopolize all your attention."

Mr. Maitland looked pointedly at Clifford. "It was a pleasure to make your acquaintance, young man," he said with finality. He held his arm out to Penelope. She took it without speaking, and they walked away.

Before they disappeared into the crowd, Penelope looked back at Clifford. She grinned and winked. He watched her enter the throng of dancers, greet a new partner and lightly dance away.

Clifford then beat a hasty retreat back to second class, relieved that his "shipboard romance" was over.

The rest of the days at sea were less eventful. Clifford spent much of his time outside on the second-class deck, strolling about or playing shuffleboard. Meals were good. They had breakfast at 8, dinner at 12:30, tea at 5:30 and supper at

8:30. The orchestra played in the second class drawing room every morning from 10 to 11. Clifford thought of Penelope when he heard a waltz. At first, he felt a twinge of guilt, but after remembering his last sight of her—giddy laugh, dancing gaily—he decided that she would do all right on her own.

When Clifford awoke on the morning of the eighth day, he could feel the ship's steam engines had slowed. He leaned over from the upper berth and peered out the small porthole. The shore line and a harbor came into view. With Allan still sound asleep, Clifford quickly hopped down from his berth, pulled on his pants and shirt, and ran up to the second-class deck.

The SS Arabic was pulling into Queenstown. He looked out at the painted fishing boats bobbing in the harbor and the colorful row houses lining the rolling coastal road. To the right of the harbor, St. Colman's Cathedral rose over the small village. It looked majestic, even with construction scaffolding surrounding the grey spire.

Passengers were allowed to disembark by showing their passports, with the warning that they would need them to board again in the evening. Clifford and Allan, glad for a change of scenery, strolled the quaint streets of the Irish town. On the outskirts, the houses had small gardens enclosed with slab stone fences. The flowers in these gardens were a tumble of bright colors, with the hydrangeas a deeper blue than Clifford had ever seen. Allan said it was because of the salt water.

The slate-roofed cottages in the more populated area of the village were built close together and whitewashed in tints of blue, yellow, pink and green. They stood so close to the street that the doors opened right out on the cobblestone walkways. Every house had window boxes bursting with blooms.

As they looked in the storefronts of the many small shops, Allan mentioned that Ireland was known for their wool, linen and lace. Clifford purchased two delicate lace handkerchiefs for his mother and Mabel. They bought bread and cheese from a street vendor and made their way to a park in the center of town. They enjoyed their lunch while people-watching from the steps of a wrought iron bandstand.

The next morning, the trip across the Irish Sea to Liverpool was rough, gales and high waves buffeted the ship. Clifford was relieved as the ship steamed up the Mersey River towards the Liverpool docks. He couldn't help but notice that the two ports couldn't have been more different. Liverpool was one of the largest ports in the world, with more than seven miles of granite and lime lagoons housing over forty wet docks.

Unlike sunny Queenstown, Liverpool seemed blanketed in a grey, misty fog.

To the north was a cluster of large commercial buildings and to the south a long line of wet docks, warehouses and cranes. Boat masts stretched along both sides of the river as far as Clifford could see, reminding him of rows of gigantic crosses in a graveyard.

The tug pushed the Arabic up alongside the Princess dock. Dock hands rushed to secure the steamer with thick, heavy lines. Below, Clifford could see throngs of men scuttling around the wide platform with paperwork for customs, invoices for cargo, and forms for port health officials.

A cacophony of sounds greeted his ears. He could hear cranes unloading cargo, the rowdy calls of workers, the banter of carters, the shouts of coach drivers, the shrill cries of flower girls and the clop of work horses' shoes on the cobblestones.

In the distance, Clifford saw terraces of hillside dwellings. Churches with their chimneys, spires and turrets silhouetted the skyline. Construction had begun on the cathedral and the dock office. The Victorian boom was as its peak.

Clifford and Allan walked the wealthy streets of Liverpool while they waited for their luggage to be unloaded. The tidy rows of stone-stepped houses, the elegant shops on Lord Street, and the high-roofed St. John's Market, which sold luxurious American goods, bore a strong resemblance to Manhattan. Clifford could see why Liverpool was called the "New York of Europe."

A few hours later, Clifford and Allan left Liverpool by the Great Western Railway for the two day journey to Dartmouth, Allan's family's home in the south of England. Clifford sat next to a window and watched the countryside roll by: Wild moors, then waterlogged Fen country with flocks of wild birds, ragged and beautiful countryside, then black smoking cities. Finally they arrived at the beautiful Devon coast. The railroad terminated at the tiny port of Kingswear. From there, they had a short easy ferry ride to Dartmouth. This beautiful little town sat on the western banks of the River Dart, nestled on a semi-circle of hills.

"My family has moved several times in the twenty years I've been gone," Allan explained to Clifford. Allan consulted his directions as he and Clifford navigated the narrow roads on foot. They followed Victoria Street, then turned on Foss St. It was an uphill climb.

St. Clément's Church stood at the top of the hill overlooking the town. Allan checked the address again and stopped in front of an attached stucco and beam Tudor house This was it. Immediately the door flung open.

"It's Allan! It's Allan!" They were immediately engulfed with bear hugs, slaps on the back, and everyone talking at once. Clifford chuckled as Allan made the introductions: Albert, Alin, Alfred, Alice, Altot, and Ali. There were a few new family members that had joined the family since Allan had gone to America: Alfred's wife Charlotte and nephews William, Charles, Cecil and George.

Allan's mother Mary sat near the hearth, out of the fray, a small fire burning to ward off the damp. The tall man bent down to give his mother a gentle kiss, then pulled up a stool to sit nearby.

Mary could not take her eyes off her son. She hung on his every word, anxious to hear firsthand about America. His letter writing was wanting. While the rest of the family listened, Allen brought his mother up to date about his work and his friends.

As first Mary nodded and smiled, but her face began to develop a frown as Allan continued. Finally she asked him, "No wife? Allan, you've not found a wife in America?"

This gave Allan pause. "Oh. Uh—" was all he said. Somehow he had reached the age of forty and had never really considered settling down.

Mary turned to Clifford. "Are there no young woman in America? Why is my Allan not married?"

Clifford grinned at Allan's discomfort, the tables turned.

"Oh, there are lots of young women in Fenton," Clifford assured Allan's mother. "Very pretty and accomplished, too. Any one of them would make Allan a good wife—if they'd have him." He grinned at his friend, who glared in return.

"What about you, Clifford?" Mary asked.

"Oh, me? I'm engaged to be married to my high school sweetheart next June."

Mary smiled at Clifford and nodded approvingly. Then she turned back to Allan, her pointed expression demanding an answer.

Allan shrugged, thinking about his situation. He roomed at a boarding house run by a widow named Hester Guest and her daughter, Margaret. He had to admit he and Margaret had lots in common. He played the accordion and she played in the Fenton Ladies Band. They spent many a pleasant evening playing bridge or 500 with Margaret's sister Fannie and her husband Ed Forte. Mags, as her family called her, was a good cook, too. But Allan liked things just as they were. He was happy being a bachelor.

Allan looked at his mother's expectant face. He turned and took in the sight of the big, lively family in the busy room. It was crowded, but warm and loving. Then another though occurred to Allan. No doubt, Margaret was waiting for him back in Fenton, wondering if he was ever going to propose. He supposed it was time.

Allan took his mother's hand and kissed her cheek again. He whispered, "You know, Mama, I suppose there is someone. You would approve. If it would make you happy I'll take care of it as soon as I return."

Clifford and Allan spent several pleasant weeks in Devonshire, traveling to meet Allan's brother and the rest of his family. There was much to see: the medieval buildings of Butterwalk; Dartmouth Castle; Kingswear Castle; Agincourt House. A new naval college was being built and Clifford and Allan could see the officers drilling on the ships from the quayside.

The beautiful sandy beaches attracted crowds of tourists. Clifford was puzzled by the many small wooden closets mounted on four large carriage wheels he saw on the beach. Allan explained that they were bathing carts. A fully dressed bather climbed into one. Then, the bathing cart was pulled by horse out into the water. Inside the cart, the swimmer changed into his or her woolen bathing outfit, and then climbed out to enjoy the water. Such modesty.

Allen had promised Clifford they'd visit London. Clifford was anxious to see the landmarks he'd learned about in history books: Buckingham Palace, Big Ben and the Tower of London. He hoped to see the changing of the guard and perhaps even a glimpse of King Edward.

They took the Holiday Line into London and looked for a respectable boarding house to lodge for a few days. They approached a white three story terraced house, in a long line of similar houses. A small window box of bright flowers was under the front parlor window. The landlady was out sweeping the front steps. Allan introduced himself and Clifford and explained they would just need a room for a few days. She looked them up and down critically.

"I run a respectable place," she said sternly. "No noise to be made in the bedrooms after 9 pm, shoes must be wiped on the map before entering, no drinking or smoking, and especially no young women!" Allan smiled.

"We understand and that will be no problem," he assured her.

She nodded. "Then it will be 5s a day for bed and a good cooked breakfast. Tea and dinner are optional, just let me know in the morning if I should expect you. Tea is at 4 pm and 1s and dinner will be an extra 2s."

Clifford and Allan nodded.

"Well, then, I'll show you to your rooms." The followed her up the front steps. She opened the front door with a gleaming brass knocker and set her broom inside.

"The sitting room is here," she motioned to the communal sitting room and then proceeded up the stairs to the second floor. The bedrooms were adequately furnished with a single bed, a chamber pot under the bed, a small cupboard with hooks for their clothes and a sturdy wooden chair. A gas light hung overhead and clean starched curtains hung at the window.

"The bathroom is at the end of the hall," the landlady said. "There's hot water but baths are on request. If you'd like a bowl and pitcher of hot water in the morning its 6d. Just let me know what time to bring it. The outhouse is out back."

The next morning, after a hearty breakfast, they headed towards the Tower of London. Clifford realized to his surprise that it was not just one big tower, as he had imagined, but a complex of buildings surrounded by a moat of water. It was an imposing sight. Across a large drawbridge over the moat was the ticket office. A squat little man sat in the ticket booth, sleeves on his work shirt rolled up to his elbows and tweed cap perched over his reddish cheeks and bulbous nose.

"Sixpence," he said. "And it will be another sixpence if ye wish to visit the Crown Jewels in the Wakefield Tower."

Clifford dug in his pocket and slid his money under the bars. The man passed him two tickets and a brochure with a drawing of the towers on the cover. They had a quarter of an hour before their tour began. Clifford sat on a stone bench to read the pamphlet.

*There is no spot in the British Isles where the memories of the past cluster more thickly than around the old grey walls, the picturesque towers and the dark and gloomy chambers of the Tower of London. Every tower reminds us of a memorable deed, every chamber of a famous name. The great fortress is peopled once more with its victors and its victims; past times live again, history ceases to be a dull record; it becomes a living moving tale.*

A shiver ran through Clifford. He looked up from the brochure and gazed at the looming stone walls. It was one thing to learn about torture and beheadings in history class. What a difference to be standing right where it all happened.

As they walked towards the start of the tour the public square where prisoners were executed was clearly visible. Clifford was shocked to learn there were still prisoners in the Tower. What a grim atmosphere.

Walking through the dark passageways, the guide told the story of the young "Princes of the Tower." Edward V and his brother Richard, Duke of York, disappeared from the tower in 1483. It was rumored that their own uncle, Richard III, had ordered their murder. Many years later, two small sets of bones were found under a stairway. Allan shook his head, "How could an uncle order the murder of his own family? Power was that important?"

The guide then took them through the Tower Green.

"This is where two of Henry VIII's queens were beheaded," the guide told them, "It was a rare honor to be beheaded inside the tower walls and not out on Tower Hill, in full view of the crowds." *Some honor,* Clifford thought. *You're dead either way.*

He was glad they had paid the extra money to see the Crown Jewels. There were over 140 objects— thirteen crowns, trumpets, maces, swords, scepters, spurs and plates. All were encrusted with jewels the like of which Clifford had never imagined—diamonds, rubies and emeralds. *Now that would be a souvenir to take home.* Suits of armor gleamed with their metal arms and hands grasping swords and lances, ready for battle. But they were certainly built for smaller men. "Allan," Clifford remarked, "How would you like to try one of these on for size?"

The tour continued with Traitor's Gate, Queen's House, the Council Chamber, Martin Tower, Salt Tower, and lastly the Bell Tower, which dated back to the 13th century.

Clifford glanced up at the huge bell. The sky was overcast and a there was a cold mist in the air. He felt as if he had been transported back in time. What an incredible day. What an incredible journey. He was so glad Aunt Julia had insisted he take this trip with Allan. For a few weeks, he had stepped out of his life in Fenton where everything was orderly and predictable and into a new and exciting world. As they finished their sightseeing Clifford insisted they stop at a souvenir stand. He bought a few postcards and several small plates painted with London landmarks but his eyes light up when he saw keys to the Tower of London for sale. Now that would be a great souvenir.

In another day, he and Allan would board the ship back to America and back to ordinary life. Clifford knew what was expected of him after graduation. He would start work at A.J. Phillips & Co, marry Mabel and live happily ever after. He was content to do so. But oh, he was so glad he had seen more of the world before he took his place in Fenton.

# 13
## *Wedding Bells*

JUNE 28, 1905

The church was beautifully decorated with palms, ferns and evergreen arches with clusters of pink roses. This marriage marked the merging of two top Fenton families: Corrigan and Phillips. Judge Corrigan was Justice of the Peace and Village President. The Phillips family ran a successful business and employed much of the townspeople. Everyone who was anyone was in attendance.

St. Jude's decorated for Mabel and Clifford's wedding

But for Mabel, peeking out at the crowd from the church anteroom, the wedding was very personal. To her, the occasion was not just a social event. She had known Clifford was "the one" since their freshman year of high school, and could hardly believe the big day—their wedding— had finally arrived.

Turning away from the doorway, Mabel nervously smoothed her gown. Her dress was white silk with a ribbed Aeolian overlay, and her tulle veil was fastened with white sweet peas. Her bouquet of white roses lay on a nearby bench.

Mabel's three bridesmaids, her friends since attending North Ward School, twittered and whispered excitedly. Dressed in pink silk with matching picture hats, they made a charming picture next to the flower girls: little Marjorie Phillips and Clifford's half-sister, Bessie Gould, both clad in white.

The girls stopped chattering when they heard organ chords. Helen Van Atta was beginning the wedding march!

Georgia Zelner, Mabel's very best friend and the maid of honor, took the hand of the ring-bearer, little Lucy Phillips, whose pink dress matched the bridesmaids'. She handed Mabel the bride's bouquet before picking up her own pink roses.

Reverend DuBois, the rector, knocked on the door. They were ready to start the ceremony.

"Are you ready?" Georgia asked.

Mabel beamed, her heart full of joy, as she took her father's arm to walk down the aisle.

St Jude's Episcopal Church. Photo courtesy of A J Phillips Historical Museum

# 14

## Bay View Club

1909

Mabel was thrilled when she was asked to join the Bay View Club soon after her wedding. As a girl, she had watched her mother put on her best afternoon dress and gloves to go to the weekly meetings. Little Mabel wondered what it would be like to be a married lady and experience the ritual of passage of being invited into the ranks. By the summer of 1909, several of her friends had joined as well. The presence of the younger women gave the Thursday afternoon meetings a boost of lively energy.

The Bay View Club meetings varied in subject matter. Many included serious discussions of current events or historical topics. Once, they had each been assigned one of Henry VIII's wives to research and discuss. For another, they had dressed as the First Ladies. Today, however, was the annual picnic. This year it was on Lake Fenton, at Mrs. Becker's handsome cottage on Lakeside Street. They gathered in the screened porch. Mrs. E.L. Becker called the meeting of the Bay View Club to order, and the club business was quickly dispatched. Luncheon was served outdoors under the shady elm trees: roast chicken, stewed tomatoes, new Bermuda potatoes, spinach, canned corn and lemon meringue pie.

After the luncheon, some of the ladies went out in the rowboat while others played croquet on the Becker's lush green lawn. Mabel, Georgia, Myrtle and Cora walked by the water's edge. With the bright sunshine and fresh air blowing in off the water, it was a beautiful afternoon on the lake.

"Oh, Mabel—look at this tree! Reminds me of the ones we climbed back when we were little. Give me a leg up," Cora said impishly.

Mabel shook her head. Cora always made everything adventurous. Would she ever grow up? But Mabel gave her friend a boost to start up the tree. Its low branches were wide and sturdy. Cora found a resting spot and looked out over the lake.

"Coming down soon? I hope you're satisfied now," Mabel remarked after a few minutes.

Cora just laughed and climbed higher.

"It's not like we're young schoolgirls any more, Cora," Mabel protested. "We're married. With children."

"Oh, so what? Come on, girls! Join me!" Cora cajoled. Mabel laughed in spite of herself, and soon the three of them joined Cora in the tree.

"I feel so silly," Mabel said as she rested against a bough.

Summer shenanigans. Photo courtesy of A J Phillips Historical Museum

"I know!" Myrtle replied. "If our husbands could see us now!"

The gentlemen were not expected until 5 PM. They had been instructed to attend in full dress. By then, the ladies would also be decked out in evening wear after their afternoon frolicking by the lake.

Mabel laughed along with the others at the thought of the menfolk coming across their young wives perched in a tree. However, looking out over the shimmering water certainly brought back memories of carefree, peaceful summer days. She relaxed against the wide tree trunk. For a little while, there were no thoughts of planning dinner, or worrying about whether her husband Clifford was happy at his job or whether their little daughter, named Nellie after Clifford's older sister, needed new shoes.

Cora's voice broke into Mabel's reverie. "We have to get a picture!" she exclaimed. "Can someone find my Kodak?"

# 15

## Phillips' Factory Fire

SEPTEMBER 14, 1914

The explosion rattled windows as far north as the house on Main Street. It startled Clifford awake. His pocket watch on the night stand read 1:45. He jumped up, grabbed his wire rim glasses and bounded over to the window. A pale red glow already illuminated the sky toward downtown. Almost immediately, the urgent sound of the steam fire whistle cut through the night. The toll of the fire bell soon joined in.

Clifford's heart sank. Shaking himself fully awake, he grabbed his pants from the wooden valet, pulled them on quickly and raised the suspenders over his shoulders. He nudged Mabel.

"It looks like there's a fire in the village. I'm going."

Mabel started to sit up, groggy with sleep. Her long brown hair hung in a thick braid down her back.

Fenton Fire Station. Photo courtesy of
A J Phillips Historical Museum.

Clifford quickly leaned over and kissed her on the forehead. "Go back to sleep. I'll be back when I can, but it looks like a big one."

He crept down the stairs carefully and hurried outside, not wanting to wake their daughter Nellie or little Jud. Their neighbor, Mr. Parker, was also heading toward town. They walked briskly, nearly running. The red glow was growing more intense. As they ran closer, they could see orange flames shooting up forty, maybe fifty feet high.

"What do you think it is?" Parker asked. "The factory?"

"Judging by the fire's size, it probably is," Clifford agreed. "All that lumber stored in the warehouse made it a tinderbox, I'm afraid. Luckily we had a sprinkling system installed a few years back when we still owned it."

Times had changed the last few years, and the property was no longer in the Phillips family. First there had been the financial panic of 1907. Automobile manufacturing began to boom as the town struggled to recover. Unfortunately, the auto industry passed Fenton by. Buick built an enormous plant in Flint. Oldsmobile and Reo set up manufacturing facilities in Lansing and Pontiac. Many of Fenton's skilled workers moved out of town, following the jobs. Even some merchants followed suit: Sol Austin sold his three-chair barbershop and relocated in Lansing; Leonard Freeman sold his creamery and set up shop in Flint. Their businesses were thriving in the new locations.

One new business did come to Fenton. The fine grey marl at the bottom of Silver Lake had brought Aetna Cement Company to the outskirts of town. Portland Cement Company soon followed. The cement companies paid $1.80 a day for twelve hours of work. A. J. Phillips & Co. could not compete with that pay rate. Their workforce dwindled.

Around the same time, Continental Company in Owosso joined a trust for the manufacturing of wood products. Soon, the trust approached A. J. Phillips & Co. with an ultimatum. It was hopeless. Within two years, Phillips had closed their doors and the property had been sold. Henry S. Koppin Interior Finish Concern now occupied the four acres of floor space. Even Clifford worked for Portland Cement Company now. Parker did, too.

As the men drew closer to downtown, they saw more and more residents hurry out of their houses. Even though Fenton had a full time fire department, a blaze this big would require as many volunteers as possible. The fire bell continued to peal urgently as the flames glowed fiercely against the black night. The general alarm was sent to Flint and Pontiac. Firebrands floated through the sky and the homes of Ed Forte and Dr. Wright were already on fire. The entire village was threatened.

Fires had been devastating to Fenton in the past. Throughout the years, destruction from fire had reshaped the village. The Bridge Fire of 1879 destroyed not only the bridge, but the stores that lined it on the east side: Anderson's cooper shop, Colwell's sawmill, the Baptist church and Fenton's Woolen Mill. In 1899, the beautiful stone three-story Baptist Ministers' Home was gutted. Latimer Hall, the Episcopal boys' school, met the same fate in 1906. Fenton finally responded by constructing the water works plant and laying water mains for the village. In addition, much new business construction was brick. This was supposed to prevent future disasters from fire. Many of the homes were still frame, however.

The heavy hose cart was pulled up as close as the horses would go and the hook and ladder truck stood at the ready. The firemen attached their hoses to the water main.

"Chief!" called one of the men. "We're not getting any water pressure."

*What in tarnation?* Clifford thought. *The sprinkling system should be working.* Then the answer occurred to him. There was not enough pressure from the water works to supply both the sprinkling system and the fire hoses.

"We have to get that sprinkler system turned off." Clifford shouted as he ran to the chief's side.

A.J. Philips & Co. Photo courtesy of A J Phillips Historical Museum

It was late morning when Clifford returned home. He sat down wearily at the kitchen table, exhausted from hours of hauling water for the bucket brigade. Soot was smeared on his face and clothes, and his hair was sweaty and mussed. As Mabel fixed rashers and eggs, he recounted the events of the night.

"The night watchman said he completed his rounds at 1 am and everything was fine. But by 1:30, the fire was discovered. It spread so rapidly that all of the factory and warehouses were lost. You won't believe it when you see it."

Mabel shook her head sadly. "Was anyone hurt?"

"Frank Plumb and Ernest Fuller suffered some bad burns."

"What happened?"

"The sprinkler system was drawing too much water from the water works and the pressure was too low for water to get to the hoses. Frank and Ernest volunteered to go in to shut the sprinklers off. They were lucky to get out alive."

Mabel sighed sympathetically as she sat down, and Clifford continued, "Well, we were able to save the Andrews' house, Galloway's plumbing and Charles Bruno's shop. So we did some good."

Clifford took a long drink of hot coffee and leaned back in his chair. "The Flint Fire Department sent their big automobile hose cart." He set the cup down. "It arrived in record time—28 minutes. What a sight."

# 16

## O E Williams
## School of Aviation

JANUARY 26, 1916

Aeroplane. Photo courtesy of A J Phillips Historical Museum

Although the automotive industry had bypassed the Village of Fenton, the town still had her suitors. O.E. Williams had come to the area on business and thought Fenton might be just the place to launch his flying school. Aeroplanes were a relatively new phenomena and the town was abuzz with excitement. A huge town meeting was planned. O.E. was equally excited, and in his excitement nearly derailed his plans.

Hurrying to get to the meeting, Williams and his chief mechanic, S.D. Robinson, decided to take a short cut from their rented cabin across Lake

Fenton and into town. The lake was frozen and dusk was falling. Whether the heavy cloud cover and setting sun obscured their vision or whether they were simply too engrossed in their plans for the meeting, Williams failed to see the markers around a patch of open water. One minute, the 1916 Saxon motorcar was running along at a good speed, her tires sliding over the glassy ice and bouncing on the occasional rough patch. The next moment the two passengers felt the thrill of weightlessness, similar to being up in one of their new aeroplanes. But only for a moment as they realized the ice had given way and their car was plummeting into the frigid water. Slowly the tires, the undercarriage, and then the doors sank.

Fortunately, the motorcar's top was down. Williams and Robinson scrambled up on top of the black leather seat. As the cold water soaked their shoes, then their pant legs, the two men looked at each other wordlessly. They weren't trapped inside the car, but they still had to escape from the lake. Was this the end of their dreams—and their lives? A cold icy death, their bodies never recovered from a dark watery grave?

Williams' mind raced as the icy water reached his knee-high garters. It had seemed like a good idea to take the shortcut across the frozen lake to get to town. Any open patches of water were clearly marked but he had failed to see the warning markers. How could he have been so stupid? He'd just paid $390 for this car!

The Saxon pitched forward and began to sink faster. Williams felt his chest constricting. The shock of the icy cold water penetrated his wool waistcoat and was making it difficult to breathe. It was now or never.

"We've got to swim!" he shouted to Robinson. Gingerly putting one foot on the top of the door, Williams pushed off, away from the sinking car, toward the edge of the hole in the ice. He grabbed for the ledge of ice but it broke off, splintering in his grasp. He could feel the weight of his soaked clothes dragging him down. Desperately, he grasped at the ledge again and again, clawing at the ice until he was able to find a firm hold. Laboriously, he slid his body up until his chest and hips lay on the cold snow-covered ice, his legs and feet still dangling in the open water. Resting only briefly, he took a few short breaths, then pulled his body forward again, now completely out of the water.

"Robinson!" Williams' voice was weak and raspy. Had he heard a reply? Pushing himself up with his arms, he scrambled upright. Robinson lay on the ice just a few yards away. Williams sighed with relief and then looked back at the water. His new car was completely submerged, with just the slightest hint of the ragtop roof above the water line. Glancing toward shore, he could see that they were just off Case's Island. There were no lights in the few cottages dotting the shoreline.

"Robinson! Quick! Quick! Get up!" urged Williams. "We have to get back to the cottage before we freeze to death!"

As Robinson struggled up, Williams took off his black hat and laid it on the white ice, quickly packing snow around it to keep it in place and mark the spot. One last look around, and the two men began trudging in the direction of the borrowed cottage. At first, they took short slow steps, then gradually quickened the pace, even as their clothes began to freeze. Williams knew they had to keep moving. He was determined to stay alive—and to attend the town meeting in Fenton.

Williams was ecstatic the next morning, even though his brand new Saxon was still at the bottom of Lake Fenton. The meeting had been a big success. What a turnout. Some said it was the biggest town meeting ever—over 150 citizens and businessmen. There were many speeches and much discussion. But when all was said and done, the Ladies Civic League agreed to secure space in the Case Manufacturing Building for Williams' business operations, at no cost. Mrs. Bussey agreed to rent the Coe plant to him for the actual manufacturing. It was the outcome he and Robinson had hoped for.

After hearing of the Saxon's demise, several men and a team of horses came out in the morning with ropes and pulleys to pull the motorcar out of the lake.

"How can we trust you to pilot an aeroplane, Williams, when you can't even handle a car?" one of them joshed. Amazingly, the only repair the Saxon needed was a new sparkplug.

# 17

# Fenton's Early Birds

## 1916

Home of Clifford & Mabel Phillips

Ten-year-old Nellie sat at the upright piano as her cat slept on the bench next to her. Her piano teacher, Miss Van Atta, had recently given her sheet music to Stephen Foster's "Beautiful Dreamer." Nellie thought it was such a lovely grown-up piece to play. She wanted to practice hard and make her parents proud of her. Concentrating intently, she didn't notice her mother at her side.

"I'm sorry to interrupt, but Uncle Ray just called," Mabel said. "He's going to watch the aeroplane pilots practice and he offered to take you with him. Do you want to go?"

Did she ever. What could be better than an afternoon with her handsome Uncle Ray, watching the aeroplanes everyone was talking about? Plus a ride in his new Chevy?

"Oh, yes, Mother," she exclaimed.

Nellie clutched Uncle Ray's hand as they crossed the large open field at Tony Dauner's farm just north of Lake Fenton. Grasshoppers jumped haphazardly from the dry weedy grass to get out of their way. Her large hair bow bouncing up and down, Nellie's legs raced to keep up with Ray's longer strides. She was so excited. Who could imagine a man going up in the sky like a bird?

Everyone was talking about the aeroplane factory in town. The first machine had been completed this past winter. It had taken both the hired workforce and a large class of student pilots working day and night to finish it. The aeroplane, which was capable of flying 90 miles per hour, had two seats and dual controls for training purposes. After successfully testing it on the ice on Lake Fenton, several more planes were built.

The pilots had been nicknamed Fenton's Early Birds. After their training was complete, they performed all over the country at exhibitions and county fairs. Today, the students were practicing takeoffs and landings. Mr. Williams himself was standing amongst them, shouting directions.

The planes were parked haphazardly on the dry grass. Most of the men wore work clothes: pants and suspenders with no jackets, sleeves rolled up and felt newsboy caps. They carried tools and greasy rags. A few others, observers from town, were dressed in business suits.

As Ray and Nellie got closer, the rumble of the motors increased. Nellie held her hand over her ears and got a good look at one of the planes. It was certainly a strange-looking machine. The aeroplane had two long wings which stretched out horizontally, and lots of wires running every which way. The pilot sat in the center of the wings, with a rudder in front to steer and the motor behind him. The entire contraption rested on three rubber wheels. Nellie saw that the propeller was made of pieces of wood glued and pressed together. Baling wire was used in many places to keep the whole thing intact, but it still appeared to be quite flimsy. Surprised, the young girl looked up at her uncle, ready to question the safety of these machines, but he was transfixed.

"Uncle Ray, are they really going to fly?" she shouted at him over the din of the motors.

"Oh, yes they are," he told her. "And someday soon I will, too."

Ray Corrigan was twenty-five years old and he was an assistant Sales Manager at Chevrolet Motor Company in Flint. He had thought working for an automotive company would be exciting. Everyone was buying cars nowadays, and he figured Chevy was the place to be. But then he discovered the aeroplane business. Now this was really something.

Two of the aviation students, Cy Bettis and Thad Johnson, roomed with Ray's parents. After dinner one evening, Cy and Thad explained all the parts of the aeroplane to the Corrigans. The stationery cross-piece was the horizontal stabilizer. The flaps across the wings were ailerons that controlled the banking. The rudder on the tail behind the vertical stabilizer controlled direction, and the flaps, called elevators, moved the nose of the plane up and down.

Ray often visited the airfield when the students practiced, and wanted nothing more than to experience flight first hand. Several weeks before, he had his chance. Cy was getting ready to go up and practice a few maneuvers.

"Hey, Ray, you want to go with me?" offered Cy, pointing to the second seat on the plane. "It'll be OK. Mr. Williams isn't here."

Without hesitation, Ray climbed in. Cy handed him a pair of goggles and a cap. "It's pretty cold up there," he warned Ray. "I'm going to turn the propeller to start the engine."

The engine clicked and popped as it fired up. As soon as it caught, Cy ran around and hopped into the pilot's seat. The plane jerked and jostled something terrible as it raced along the rough field, gathering speed. Suddenly, Ray felt the calm as the ground dropped beneath them. He was flying. He looked out in amazement at the farmland below. The neatly plowed rows of corn and wheat made striped patterns on the ground. The trees dotting the hedgerows that divided the fields quickly shrunk to the size of bushes. Soon, they were over Fenton and Ray could pick out individual houses. Folks had become accustomed to hearing the drone of the aeroplanes overhead, but the children looked up, pointing and waving.

Ray wondered what his girlfriend, Clara Forte, would think if she looked up. Would she be able to tell that it was him? He knew she wasn't wild about Ray's desire to fly, but she hadn't voiced any objection. Ray's parents, however, were very much against the idea—too dangerous, they insisted.

As they gained altitude, the air became more turbulent. Ray hung on and thought about another reason to take up flying. For the last two years, a war had raged in Europe after the assassination of Archduke Ferdinand. At first, it seemed merely a local skirmish. But German subs had been sinking merchant ships in the Atlantic. The Lusitania and the SS Arabic had been sunk, causing a diplomatic incident. There was talk that President Woodrow Wilson might take action, and some people thought America's involvement was inevitable.

Ray had even heard talk that the Army would use aeroplanes in battle. If America joined the war that's where he wanted to serve.

# 18
## World War

1918

Once a week, Ray came from his rented room in Flint to visit his parents, C.L. and Minnie Corrigan for dinner. It had become his habit to stop by the post office on his way. Since the United States had entered the war in April and Congress had passed the Selective Service Act, all men his age were required to register for the draft. Ray had registered immediately, but was still waiting to be called.

The draft notices were posted on the wall outside the post office, tacked over the previous week's listing which had turned yellow and tattered in the elements. Ray scanned the narrow columns of newsprint, just as he had done many times before. He was surprised to see his name posted. Finally, after all these weeks. He read it again just to be sure it was real. He was to report to Fort Wayne, Indiana in two weeks.

Ray was anxious to do his part for his

Ray Corrigan and his "Jenny"

country, but he wanted to do it in the newly formed Air Service of the army, not as a doughboy. He knew the Air Service accepted only exceptional candidates. He hoped they would take him.

---

To:     Miss Clara Forte
        105 W. Caroline Street
        Fenton, Michigan
From:   Ray Corrigan
        Camp Dix, New York

February 29, 1918

Dearest Clara,

Just wanted to let you know I arrived here at Camp Dix this afternoon. I'm assigned a cot in a big white tent with quite a few other guys. There's row after row of tents, like a city. We all hope to qualify for pilot training. There's a lot of competition so wish me good luck. We begin testing in the morning. I heard there are all kinds of physical tests for endurance, reaction time, breathing capacity, color vision and equilibrium. If I pass, then I'll start the ground school training right here at Cornell. Well, I'm pretty beat from the train ride and need to get settled in. I miss you terribly. I'll let you know how I do. If I pass I'll be stationed here for awhile. We can make our plans as soon as I know.

*Love, Ray*

To:     Miss Clara Forte
        105 W. Caroline Street
        Fenton, Michigan
From:   Ray Corrigan
        Camp Dix, New York

March 1, 1918

Dearest Clara,

I passed! It wasn't as difficult as I had been led to believe, but we are told the tough part begins now. We'll learn radio communications, gunnery, engine control, and airplane inspection—all in the classroom. I can't wait to get the book work out of the way and actually start flying. That's the good news. The bad news is we also have to learn the soldiering part of the business—how to march, salute, stand in formation and shoot. No one likes that part of the training and to be honest, I don't think we're terribly good at it.

I enjoy your letters more than you know. Despite being with hundreds of guys, it's pretty lonely. I can hardly wait another month until your visit. I've spoken to the minister at St. John's Church and made arrangements for the ceremony. I know it won't be the wedding you've dreamed of, with only your parents as witnesses, but the important part is we will be husband and wife.

Well, I've got lots of studying to do. Be sure to give my best to your parents

*Love, Ray*

To:     Ray Corrigan
        Camp Dix, New York
From:   Miss Clara Forte
        105 W. Caroline Street
        Fenton, Michigan

March 24, 1918

My dear Ray,

What a relief that you could make the arrangements with the minister. I'm sure there are many young couples like us who want to tie the knot before the guys are sent overseas. I miss you desperately and I can't wait to see you again. Mother is so excited. She bought a new hat and dress in Detroit. It set Dad back $32.20. I guess she just can't believe I'm finally getting married. I'd tell you all about my dress, but you know that would be bad luck, so you'll just have to be surprised. Pleasantly surprised, I hope.

How is your training going? Now that you boys have left its pretty dull here. Sometimes it's hard to remember there's even a war going on. Mabel, Edna and I went to the Rowena to see "Tarzan of the Apes" starring Elmo Lincoln and Enid Markey. It was very entertaining and it keeps our mind off this terrible war. Do you get much news about the war? We heard there was a big battle between the Germans and the British, and it was not good news. The only bright spot is our upcoming trip to see you. We should arrive Friday about 11 am. I can't wait for our big day

*Love always, Clara*

Night letter to Mr. and Mrs. C.L. Corrigan
      Fenton, Michigan
From:   Ray Corrigan
      Ithaca, New York
March 30, 1918
    Clara and I married today in St. John's Church STOP Love Ray STOP


To:     Margaret Gunning
      303 Ellen Street
      Fenton, Michigan
From:   Fannie Forte
      Clinton Hotel
      116 N. Cayuga Street
      Ithaca, New York
April 1, 1918

My dear sister Margaret,

It's been quite a trip and I am wore out. The train ride was over 24 hours from Fenton to Detroit to Buffalo and then finally Ithaca. Ray put us up at the Clinton Hotel and gave us a tour of the university grounds. Cornell has a beautiful campus. On Saturday, Clara and Ray were married at St. John's Church at 5:30. It was a nice little wedding. Afterwards, we went to dinner at the hotel. Sunday we all went to Easter services and then took a long auto drive, about 40 miles, with two of Ray's friends. Ray had to return to camp Monday, but we went with Clara and saw the boys drill at Camp Dix. It's amazing how the camp has sprung up. It has many two-story frame buildings and row after row of white tents—practically its own city. The tents are quite large. They sleep eight to twelve men. Oh Mags, this really brings the war home. When we saw all the boys leaving on the train in Fenton they were our sons and neighbors, dressed in civilian clothes and full of vim and vigor. Seeing the young men at camp, in uniform, marching in formation, they're soldiers now. Almost everyone is dressed in their brown uniforms and campaign hats, and so often rifles in hand. I worry so, not just for Ray but all the boys, all our sons and nephews. Tomorrow we head for Philadelphia. I'll write again.

*Love, Fannie*

To:     Fannie Forte
        Clinton Hotel
        Ithaca, New York
From:   Margaret Gunning
        303 Ellen Street
        Fenton, Michigan

My dearest sister Fannie,

    I know you're moving around so I hope this letter finds you before you come home to Fenton, but Allan and I just wanted to convey our congratulations to Clara and Ray. Please tell my niece how happy we are for her. I ran into Minnie Corrigan at the post office and she told me they had received the night letter. They are thrilled, too, and sorry they were not there. We will have to celebrate when they are back in town.

*Love, Mags*

To:     Margaret Gunning
        303 Ellen Street
        Fenton, Michigan
From:   Fannie Forte
        Martinique Hotel
        49 W. 32nd Street
        New York, New York

April 8, 1918

My dear sister Mags,

    Our grand adventure continues. Clara, Ed and I took the train to Philadelphia on Monday. It's a pity Clara and Ray can't have a proper honeymoon. They will have to wait until after the war. We did some shopping and I bought a few things for Clara. We had lunch at the YMCA. Friday, we went back to Camp Dix and then Ed and I left for New York City on Sunday. It was so hard to say goodbye to Clara. We did a little shopping on 5th Avenue and then saw Charlie Chaplin's new movie at the Rialto, "It's a Dog's Life." We're staying at a nice hotel, the Martinique on 49 West and 32nd Street. You remember the Scofields? They are staying at the Whittier Hotel. We plan to see them this afternoon and then attend evening services at St. Bartholomew's. We will be coming home on the Wolverine at 5 PM. See you then.
    Our love to you and Allan,

*Your sister, Fannie*

To:     Clara Forte Corrigan
        105 W. Caroline
        Fenton, Michigan
From:   Ray Corrigan
        Camp Dix
        Ithaca, New York

May 3, 1918

Dearest Clara,

How is everything back in Fenton? I have some exciting news. Uncle Sam is sending me to California. My flight training will be at Rockwell Field in San Diego. I'll be there at least six weeks, maybe longer, until I get my commission. I will let you know my new address as soon as I get there. It was sure great being home and seeing everybody, especially you. I miss you so much. Have you seen a copy of the flash picture they took at the family dinner?

*Love, Ray*

Left to right: Top row: Clifford Phillips, Mabel Phillips, Ray Corrigan, Clara Corrigan, Margaret Guest Gunning, Edna Enevich. Middle row: Amelia (Fannie) Forte, Minnie Corrigan, Ed Forte, C L Corrigan. Bottom row: Nellie Phillips, two unidentified boys and Juddy Phillips

To:     Ray Corrigan
        Rockwell Field
        San Diego, California
From:   Clara Forte Corrigan
        105 W. Caroline Street
        Fenton, Michigan

May 8, 1918

My dear Ray,

I sure do have a copy of that picture—all the family together and you in your uniform right in the center. It's framed and sitting on my dressing table. You look so handsome in it. And now you're in California. San Diego is not too far from Berkley. I believe Burns Fuller is still out there, unless he's in the army, too. I'm sure he'd like to see you. When I visited with my family in 1911, he took me all around Oakland and San Francisco. I know you probably don't have much time off but if you do you really need to see Golden Gate State Park, the Cliff House and Seal Rocks. The one thing I remember from that trip is all the flowers— calla lilies in hedges, poinsettias, date palms and the orange groves. I know you're there for training, but hopefully you can enjoy some of the sights, too. We had a fearful storm here last night. Mother and I went out this morning to see the damage. There were lots of tree limbs down and a few broken windows. I've been playing the organ at church and busy with choir practice. Other than that not too much is exciting here.

*Love, Clara*

To:     Clara Forte Corrigan
        105 W. Caroline Street
        Fenton, Michigan
From:   Ray Corrigan
        Rockwell Air Field
        San Diego, California

May 10, 1918

Dearest Clara,

I'm here in San Diego and settled in. There are only 5 fellas in my class and they started us training right off. We start the day with book work and then fly with the instructor for about a half hour twice a day. The plane is called a Jenny, although its official name is a Curtiss JN-4A. At first we just learned how to taxi on the ground, but now we're taking off and landing. It's so noisy up there we had to learn hand signals so the instructor can communicate with us. Can you believe it, darling? I'm finally flying! I wish you could see me. I'm afraid I won't have time to look up our old friend Burns, but if I do, I'm going to remind him that you're taken!

*Yours, Ray*

To:     Clara Forte Corrigan
        105 W. Caroline Street
        Fenton, Michigan
From:   Ray Corrigan
        Rockwell Field
        San Diego, California
May 17, 1918

Dearest Clara,

Training is going great. I always knew I was meant to fly. They can teach all the theory they want, but I really feel you either have the knack or you don't, and I guess I do. I learned to do figure eights and now we're learning to glide and climb. You won't believe how high I've been. I hope I can take you up with me one day. You'd love it. We're getting some experience in mechanics, too. Even though they have mechanics to take care of the Jennys, it's still the pilot's responsibility to make sure everything is shipshape before we go up. That's all right with me. Heck, it's my neck on the line, right? I've always loved tinkering with engines and the Jenny's just a glorified car engine. Well, a really fast car. She's 8 cylinder and 90 horsepower.

*All my love, Ray*

To:     Clara Forte Corrigan
        105 W. Caroline Street
        Fenton, Michigan
From:   Ray Corrigan
        North Island
        San Diego Bay, California
May 28, 1918

Dearest Clara,

I've been sent to a little training facility in San Diego Bay called North Island. It's sure not much, just a flat, sandy island about 4 miles long and 2 miles wide. All that's here is a couple of open-sided hangars, a dusty runway and an operations office. But here's where the real flying begins. It's all solo now. I'll be flying cross country in a big triangle. Each leg is at least 30 miles. After that, I have at least 2 straight flights 75 miles out and back. I couldn't ask for a better job. We're just anxious to be sent overseas and get in the thick of things.

*Love, Ray*

To:     Clara Forte Corrigan
        105 W. Caroline Street
        Fenton, Michigan
From:   Ray Corrigan
        North Island
        San Diego Bay, California
June 10, 1918

Dearest Clara,

How are you feeling? I think about you often and hope everything is all right. I try not to worry. When you're flying, you can't let your thoughts wander. You won't believe what they have us doing. We're back with the instructor in the plane and it's a good thing. They call it Flying Acrobatics and to tell the truth I feel like I could be a barnstormer. We're learning how to recover from stalls, make loops and spiral dives. After we perfect those moves, we'll learn to fly in formation in groups of four. Then we each need at least 20 hours of solo time. It's incredible up in the sky all alone. I can't even describe the feeling!

*Love, Ray*

To:    Clara Forte Corrigan
        105 W. Caroline
        Fenton, Michigan
From:  Ray Corrigan
        Rockwell Field
        San Diego, California

July 3, 1918

Dearest Clara,

Congratulate me! I made it! I passed my RMA and I've got my patch and silver wings to prove it. I won't lie. The final tests were grueling. We had to land on a mark with the motor idling and then again with the motor dead. The first time we practiced that I thought my heart would stop. But once you learn how to use the weight of the plane to glide in, it's not so bad. And truthfully, now I feel like I'm prepared for just about anything up there. I wish I could say training was over but now we go on to Advanced Flight Training. I'll be assigned to learn one of the following: pursuit, observation or bombardment. The instructors have tried to tell us observation is the most important job of the air command but everyone I know, including me, is hoping to be assigned to pursuit. Like the song says, soon this Yank will be "Over There." Look out, Red Baron!

*Yours, Ray*

To:    Ray Corrigan
        Rockwell Field
        San Diego, California
From:  Clara Forte Corrigan
        105 W. Caroline Street
        Fenton, Michigan

July 8, 1918

My dear Ray,

Congratulations! I'm busting my buttons! I can't wait to tell everyone you passed your flight training. I telephoned to tell your parents and Mabel and Clifford right away. Mabel wanted me to tell you how proud she is of her little brother. We are all so proud of you. Your dream has finally come true. I can't help but worry a little about the flying stunts you're learning. It sounds so dangerous. I'm feeling better now. Dr. Gould called it morning sickness. He said it was common in my condition and not to worry. For quite a while I could hardly stand to be in the kitchen. But now food sounds awfully good and I try to help Mother when I can. Usually I get dinner for us all after Sunday services. The 4th of July was really something this year. It started with a big Red Cross parade and then a picnic. I think the whole town turned out. Mother and her friends at the Red Cross have worked for months to pull this off and it was a huge success! She hasn't finished the book-keeping, but it looks like the ladies raised over $2,000. I want all you boys to know how hard the ladies back home are working to do their part. There was a speaker from Michigan Agricultural College at the last Guild Meeting. She gave us tips for gardening and canning. Everyone has planted Liberty Gardens and we've been asked to observe Meatless Mondays and Wheat-less Wednesdays so more food can go to the troops. Mother and her friends are at the Red Cross rooms in the Village Center several times a week knitting sweaters, mufflers, and helmet liners. Everyone back home wants to help however we can. Be careful up in the sky!

*Your loving wife, Clara*

To:      Ray Corrigan
         Rockwell Field
         San Diego, California
From:   Clara Forte Corrigan
         105 W. Caroline Street
         Fenton, Michigan

July 27, 1918

My dear Ray,

    Boy oh boy, is it hot here! Mother says I'm just feeling the heat more in my condition. I guess I shouldn't complain to you. It's probably even hotter in California. Last week I went out to Lake Fenton with Alice Van Atta and yesterday Mother, Dad and I went out to the Phillips' cottage. It's so nice and cool out there. I love being by the water and watching the boats. For a few hours, I can forget about the war. The church picnic is set for August 13th this year at Bay Point. We're expecting about 100 people from both the church and Sunday school. I'm looking forward to that.

*Love, Clara*

To:     Clara Forte Corrigan
        105 W. Caroline St
        Fenton, Michigan
From:   Ray Corrigan
        Rockwell Field
        San Diego, California

July 29, 1918

Dearest Clara,

   I am pleased to report that you are no longer married to a lowly enlisted man. I received my commission today and I'm now a Second Lieutenant. I'll be home in a couple weeks and then I'll be stationed at Call Field. That's in Texas. The best part is you can join me there if you're feeling up to the trip. I'm not sure how long we'll be there, though. They've asked me to consider becoming an instructor. I'd prefer to be trained in pursuit but under the circumstances I guess I need to think about you and the baby. If I decide to take it, we may be moving on to Hampton Va.

                                                          Love, Ray


To:     Ray Corrigan
        Rockwell Field
        San Diego, California
From:   Clara Forte Corrigan
        105 W. Caroline Street
        Fenton, Michigan

August 9, 1918

My dear Ray,

   I can't wait to see you in your new uniform. You must look so dashing. I've already started packing so I can join you in Texas. Your parents stop by often, and Mabel and Clifford, too. They're all excited about the baby. Other than that, it's pretty quiet. I go with Mother sometimes to play 500 or bridge with Aunt Margaret and Edna. I can't wait for this war to be over and to have you home.

                                                          Love, Clara

To:    Clara Forte Corrigan
       Call Field, Texas
From: Fannie Forte
       105 W. Caroline Street
       Fenton, Michigan

September 23, 1918

Dear Clara,

It was wonderful having Ray home, but now that you've both left, the house is so quiet. I hope you like it in Texas. You will come home when it's time for the baby, won't you? I've been keeping busy doing lots of canning and sewing up at the Red Cross. Mags and I went to the movie "Shoulder Arms" with Charlie Chaplin. We've been asked to conserve gasoline now by not driving the car one day a week. Your dad and I chose Sunday so no more Sunday afternoon drives. It's a small sacrifice and one we're only too happy to make for the cause. Aunt Mags and Uncle Allan send their best.

*Love, Mother*

To:    Fannie and Ed Forte
       105 W. Caroline Street
       Fenton, Michigan
From: Clara Forte Corrigan
       Langley Field
       Hampton, Virginia

October 3, 1918

Dear Mother and Dad,

Ray and I have packed up and moved again! We are at Langley Field in Hampton, Virginia. Although Ray really wanted to learn pursuit and be in the thick of the war, he decided with the baby coming he should take the Army's offer to become an instructor. I am so relieved, although if he has to go up with the new pilots in training that may not be much safer. Ray says the war is going well and may be over soon. We can only hope and pray.

*Love, Clara*

To:      Clara and Ray Corrigan
         Langley Field
         Hampton, Virginia
From:    Fannie Forte
         105 W. Caroline Street
         Fenton, Michigan

October 29, 1918

Dear Clara and Ray,

Hope all is well with you both. Thank you for the birthday card and $3. You are so thoughtful. There was a big demonstration here last week over Germany's surrendering. It went on until 4 AM. I can't remember when I've been up that late but nobody wanted to go home. What a relief to have an end to this horrible war. Now we just have this flu epidemic to worry about. Is it bad where you are? Last week the schools and theaters were closed because so many people were sick. Over 300 cases of the flu were reported. It is fearful. At least ten people in town have died. There were three funerals just today.

*Love, Mother*

To:      Clara Forte Corrigan
         Langley Field
         Hampton, Virginia
From:    Fannie Forte
         105 W. Caroline Street
         Fenton, Michigan

November 5, 1918

Dear Clara,

Your dad wanted me to be sure to thank you and Ray for the box of cigars and nice letter you sent him for his birthday. 67! Time sure does fly. We are so looking forward to you all being here for Christmas.

*Love, Mother*

To:     Air Service Squad 6
        Taliaferro Field
        Hicks, Texas
From:   Ray Corrigan
        105 W. Caroline Street
        Fenton, Michigan

November 16, 1918

Dear Guys,

Clara and I are back in Fenton. It will be a short visit for me, but Clara will be staying until the baby is born. I don't know how you and the guys celebrated the signing of the peace treaty, but we did it up right here. I was glad I was home for the festivities. There was a big jubilee in town and the streets were packed. I'm guessing there were over 3,000 people and all had a big and glorious time. I'll be back to Taliaferro Field next week and will see you and the guys then. I'm looking forward to receiving our "Certificate of Graduation" from the Air Service Flying School. Hope you haven't smashed up all the Jennys while I've been gone. It's too hard to get parts!

*Ray*

To:     Ray Corrigan
        Taliaferro Field
        Hicks, Texas
From:   Clara Forte Corrigan
        105 W. Caroline Street
        Fenton, Michigan

November 28, 1918

My dear Ray,

This is our first Thanksgiving as husband and wife and we're not even together. Your parents were here with Aunt Margaret and Uncle Allan. We had a wonderful turkey dinner and now we are going up to Edna's to play bridge this evening. I hope you received the candy I made for you. It looks like we might be getting a storm tonight. Oh, and you won't believe we just heard Mrs. Laura Rolland died of the dreadful flu yesterday.

*Love, Clara*

To:     Clara Forte Corrigan
        105 W. Caroline Street
        Fenton, Michigan
From:   Ray Corrigan
        Taliaferro Field
        Hicks, Texas

December 5, 1918

Dearest Clara,

I missed you for Thanksgiving, too. Guess I missed you all so much I ended up in the hospital! An army hospital is not the place you want to spend a holiday. Fortunately I just had a touch of something and I'm feeling a lot better now. Will be home in time for Christmas anyway!

*Love, Ray*


To:     Air Service Squad 6
        Taliaferro Field
        Hicks, Texas
From:   Ray Corrigan
        105 W. Caroline Street
        Fenton, Michigan

January 1, 1919

Dear Guys,

Just thought I'd let you know I got a few extra days of leave before I report back. We had a white Christmas here with sleighs out and everything, something our Texas buddies probably can't even imagine. I've got big news! Our daughter was born December 29th! I couldn't have asked for a better Christmas present. We named her Margaret and she is the prettiest thing. Guess I'm just a proud papa. Hope you had a good Christmas, too, but I bet you can't beat that!

*Ray*

# PART 3

## The Scotts

# Scott Family Tree

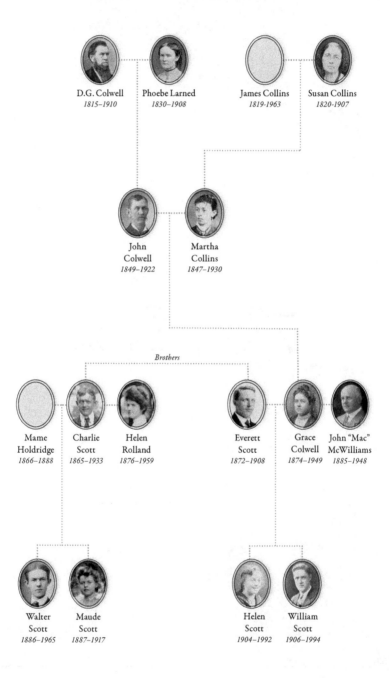

D.G. Colwell
1815–1910

Phoebe Larned
1830–1908

James Collins
1819-1963

Susan Collins
1820-1907

John
Colwell
1849–1922

Martha
Collins
1847–1930

*Brothers*

Mame
Holdridge
1866–1888

Charlie
Scott
1865–1933

Helen
Rolland
1876–1959

Everett
Scott
1872–1908

Grace
Colwell
1874–1949

John "Mac"
McWilliams
1885–1948

Walter
Scott
1886–1965

Maude
Scott
1887–1917

Helen
Scott
1904–1992

William
Scott
1906–1994

# 19

## Kicked off the Train

### 1883

Fenton Train Station. Photo courtesy of A J Phillips Historical Museum

---

Thump- thump! Thump- thump! Charlie Scott sat slumped behind the cargo crates in the far corner of the wooden rail car. He had chosen a boxcar in the middle of the train, not too close to the engine and yet away from the caboose and the train security guard. The car was cold and dark, and the floor was hard. He didn't think he'd be able to sleep, but the rhythmic vibrations of the metal wheels on the rails eventually caused him to doze off.

Charlie was already exhausted when he hopped the train just outside of Capac early that morning. He was leaving the hardscrabble life of the farm for good. Many men enjoyed tilling the soil, tending to the animals, planting, weeding, and harvesting. Not Charlie. Hard work didn't bother him, but the dirt, the smells, and the dependence on the infernal weather sure did. The uncertainty was maddening. A farmer toiled all year long, but if there was too little or too much rain, if there was hail or if disease swept through the crop, then the hard work was all for naught.

The more successful farmers mechanized. Tractors, harrowers and plows made their work less backbreaking, but Charlie's pa could not afford modern equipment. Some farmers borrowed money for machinery and when they could not afford to repay their loan, they lost everything. Pa Scott wanted no part of that. Besides, he insisted that the horse and plow served them well enough.

In addition to the risks and endless labor that came with farming, crop prices had been falling for the last ten years. There seemed to be no end in sight to the downturn. Charlie's pa blamed the railroad owners, the grain elevator operators, the bankers and the politicians for his misfortune.

Regardless of blame, Charlie had had enough. Excited to discover opportunities outside the small farm and its hardships, he couldn't wait to get away. Charlie hadn't made the decision against his father's wishes, however. He had talked to his pa about leaving. As much as William Scott could ill afford to lose a good worker, the small farm could no longer support his family: seven children and still growing. Since Charlie was of the age to be taking a wife and starting his own family, his pa reluctantly agreed it was best if he struck out on his own.

After the new year of 1883 had been rung in, Charlie was anxious to set off. However, George, Stephan and Everett would be obliged to pick up Charlie's share of the chores once he was gone. Not wanting to leave his brothers in a bind, he agreed to wait almost the full year, until after the next season's crops had been brought in and stored for the winter. For their part, the girls helped their mother with cooking, cleaning, laundry, and caring for three-year-old Floyd.

So Charlie stayed through the spring, tilling and planting. He endured the summer weeding and haying with the hot sun on his back, and he helped harvest the corn and wheat while dreaming of a very different life.

Finally, come fall, Charlie hopped a train outside of town. The Detroit, Grand Haven and Milwaukee Rail Road ran through Durand to Detroit, and he hoped to ride all the way to the city. He felt sure that his future was there. The town of Capac was only a couple of wooden buildings. Detroit was a big unknown, but it was bound to have untold opportunities for a hard worker.

The blast of the steam brakes slowing the train and the screech of the metal woke him. Could they be in Detroit already? As the train slowed, Charlie could hear the soft hiss of the steam from the engine, the clang of the train bell and the general murmur of activity outside. He stayed put, hopefully hidden from the train watchman. If this was Detroit, they would be here for some time while the cargo was unloaded. Then Charlie would find a chance to sneak out.

Charlie listened closely as the watchman inspected the boxcars. He heard several loud raps from a nightstick, then a grind as each boxcar door was rolled open. He could tell the guard was coming closer and shrank back in the shadows, hoping to remain undetected. Suddenly, the door to his car rolled open and light poured in.

"Hey, you!" the watchman barked.

He had been spotted.

A burly man, the guard's three-piece navy suit with brass buttons strained against his girth. Beads of perspiration dotted his full, flushed face underneath a small, stiff-brimmed hat. Rapping his stick swiftly on the floor of the car, the guard shouted again. "Out with ya!"

Charlie sprang up. His muscles were cramped after sitting uncomfortably, but he knew better than to hang around. The dangers of hopping a ride on even a slow-moving train were great: falling under the moving wheels, wrenching an arm, getting rolled by vagrants. But the injuries from a beating by the security guard were even greater. He high-tailed it to the opening, dropped to the floor of the car and jumped down onto the tracks.

Perhaps the guard was at the end of his shift, or perhaps he recognized Charlie as an inexperienced farm boy and not a professional vagabond riding the rails. Whatever the reason, he shouted and shook his fist but made little effort to chase Charlie as he sprinted away. Ducking between the waiting carriages and flat-bottomed wagons being loaded with supplies, Charlie ran until he felt he was out of the watchman's view.

Once he felt safe, he stopped and surveyed his surroundings, breathing heavily. The town was bigger than Capac, but even inexperienced Charlie could tell it was not Detroit. The Gothic Revival-style train station with its steep gables, arched cornices and stepped frieze, looked newly built. At the top of the gable was a round window. Sure enough, below the window was a sign that read "Fenton." This was not the big city. Not by a long shot.

A wooden platform ran parallel to the tracks. Several workmen and their empty wagons waited on the platform for their supplies. Other men stood near the station house, well-dressed in suits and felt hats. No one paid any attention to Charlie. He paused, slid his hands in his dungarees and kept his eyes on the ground as he slunk away, feeling defeated. Now what?

The railroad station was on the north side of town. Charlie headed south, towards the business district. The dirt roads were wide, with hitching posts at the store fronts and watering troughs. Jump-seat surreys, spring wagons and long, flat hay wagons drove by. Charlie gaped in amazement as he walked. This wasn't Detroit, but it sure was busier than tiny Capac.

Leroy Street was lined with all sorts of stores. Many were brick, two stories tall. The walkways in front of the stores were cobblestone. Charlie peered in the window of Corrigan's Dry Goods and saw that they sold not just food items and tools, but cloth, millinery, and shoes. He had never seen such an array.

It was a good time for Fenton. Recently, local businessmen had banded together to give A.J. Phillips a $1,000 bonus to expand his manufacturing facility. The Normal School in Milford had started an Episcopal girls' school, Ridley Hall, in the northeast section of the village. The Colwell Opera House was being renovated. The village was booming.

As Charlie came to the end of Leroy Street, the area became more residential. The cobblestone walkways became wood plank. The homes were large and nicely painted with curtains in the windows and flowers out front. Such a contrast to the weathered grey farmhouse and hard packed dirt yard he'd left behind. *No chickens scratching in the dust here*, he thought.

Soon Charlie's rumbling stomach reminded him he hadn't eaten since morning. He had no coins in his pocket, since Pa didn't pay cash wages to his sons. He told them that having a roof over their heads and food to eat was pay enough. Charlie pondered his options, then noticed one particular house on the corner.

A young girl was working in the side yard. The laundry she hung on a clothesline swayed gently in the fall breeze. Charlie watched, wondering if he dared approach her. Maybe she would be kind enough to give him some bread.

At home he knew everyone, at least to say hello. Not that there were many people to know in a tiny farm town. Most everyone gathered at church on Sunday mornings, but Pa didn't care much for preaching.

Even when Charlie did talk to people, speech did not come easily. He could never get the words out quite right. No one cared much at home when he struggled to speak, but here? How could he talk to a stranger, especially a young girl?

Hesitant, Charlie continued to stare. The girl was dressed in a neat cotton dress, with a crisp starched white apron and cap, not the rough homespun his ma and sisters wore. Charlie then noticed another woman out in the yard, playing with a young boy in the grass. The woman was very pretty. She wore a light grey dress with a lace overlay on the bodice. A necklace with a locket set off the contrasting trim on the high collar. Her dark wavy hair was piled up on her head, away from her face. Speaking occasionally to the child, she leisurely went about her work, cutting rhododendrons and gathering them in large bunches. The little group made for a lovely, tranquil picture. Charlie was transfixed.

The woman must have felt Charlie's gaze. Suddenly, she raised her head and turned, momentarily startled to find someone watching her. She wasn't frightened, however. The train station was a short distance to the north, and vagrants often wandered by, looking for a meal before they moved on. They usually found one at this home.

In a friendly tone, the woman called out to the young man. "Can I help you?"

Her voice and the grumblings from Charlie's stomach shook him out of his trance. He nodded and she motioned for him to come closer. Charlie walked into the side yard of the neatly painted, two-story house. He noticed the intricate dental molding and corbels painted in contrasting yellow and green. The girl hanging clothes turned and glanced at him briefly, but then went back to her work.

Often when Charlie spoke words just did not come out quite right. No one cared much at home. Charlie remained silent so the woman spoke again. "You look hungry. You're welcome to come in and have something to eat." Hesitant, Charlie continued to stare. She picked up the little boy and motioned for Charlie to follow her up the steps to a side porch, then inside.

Charlie found himself in a bright, clean kitchen. Another woman was chopping vegetables at a counter next to a large cast iron sink which was equipped with a hand pump for water. She was dressed like the girl outside: a cotton dress with an apron and small cap. In the middle of the kitchen was a wooden table with an oilcloth cover and several wooden chairs. A gleaming cast iron nickel-plated cook stove stood against the wall and bright copper pots and pans hung above it. At home, they brought in water from the well outside and cooked over the open fireplace. Charlie had never seen a kitchen like this. His Ma and the girls would not believe it!

The lady motioned for Charlie to sit down. "Cook," she instructed, "can you get out the cold chicken from last night for—" She paused. "What did you say your name was? I'm Mrs. Corrigan, Mary, but everyone calls me Minnie." She bounced the little boy on her hip. "This is Colin. He's three." The child grinned at Charlie. Dressed in a full gown with puffy sleeves, lace and tiny buttons down the back, the only giveaway that he was a boy was the center part of his hair.

Charlie gulped nervously. "I-I-I-I'm Ch-Ch-Charlie. Sc-Scott." he managed to stammer.

Minnie appeared to take no notice of his difficulty. She smiled warmly. "How nice. My husband's name is Charles, too, but we call him C.L."

Charlie looked around from his seat at the table. Past the green pie safe in the kitchen, he could see a dining room with patterned wallpaper on both the walls and ceiling. A chandelier hung from an ornate medallion. In the center of the room, a red and white flowered carpet covered the floor underneath a mahogany dining table with eight matching chairs. In the corner, a built- in china cabinet with glass doors was filled with china and crystal.

Minnie sat in the kitchen chair opposite Charlie. She placed her little son, Colin, on the floor by her feet and smiled as Cook set a plate of cold chicken and fresh hot biscuits in front of the young man. Minnie was a Christian woman who took to heart the preacher's admonition to visit the sick, feed the hungry and help the poor. She had grown up on Detroit's affluent Canfield Street, the daughter of the Superintendent of Western Union. Their home was an impressive brick Victorian with a wraparound porch. Canfield was a cobblestone and brick road, 100 feet wide and lined with beautiful shade trees. The families on Canfield represented the moral, religious, civic and business conscience of Detroit—Social Register people. In fact, the street was nicknamed "Piety Row."

Minnie's convictions were not for show, however. She truly possessed a kind and giving nature. Her husband, C.L., often told her she was too soft-hearted, but he did not begrudge her habit of helping strangers. He owned a dry goods store in town. It was cash on the barrel only—no credit. C.L. claimed this was the way to keep prices low. Minnie felt very fortunate that the business was doing well, but ached for her neighbors when they could not afford what they needed.

She watched Charlie eat, noticing that his meager belongings were wrapped in a cloth. Although his clothing was worn, he was clean and polite. What circumstances had brought him to Fenton?

When the plate was empty, Cook brought hot coffee. Charlie relaxed a bit while he drank. He tried to answer's Minnie's gentle questions without stammering, explaining that he had left his father's farm in Capac to seek a better life, and that he was looking for work. When he had finished his second cup of coffee, he stood up to leave. "Thank you very much, Ma'am," he said, moving toward the kitchen door, "You've been most kind."

Minnie stood as well. "Just a minute," she said. "Are you willing to do a few odd jobs to earn your meal? If you do well, you can stay for supper." Charlie nodded, happy for the opportunity.

Minnie instructed Charlie to clean out the flower beds for winter, and he started in with rake and hoe. Fat end-of-summer flies flew lazily. Bees crawled in and out of the still-bright fall blooms. The work was somewhat like farming, but not so bad when his stomach was satisfied and he had the promise of another good meal at the end of the day. As he raked, Charlie could hear Minnie playing with Colin on the side porch, and also the sound of a baby waking in a bedroom upstairs.

Minnie watched Charlie toiling in the flower beds, and had an idea. Her husband had spent five years building Corrigan's Dry Goods into a thriving business, despite the occasional competition from other stores. It provided them with a very comfortable living. But she knew he had other ambitions. He enjoyed discussing local politics with his customers. He loved to hear about the world beyond Fenton and traveled often to Detroit, coming home with stories of the huge new Brooklyn Bridge in New York City, the Statue of Liberty's dedication by President Grover Cleveland, and the Washington Monument— the tallest building in the world!— finally being completed. If he had some help in the store, it would give him more time to devote to these other interests. She knew he had his eye set on a political position, Justice of the Peace, perhaps. Minnie heard baby Mabel waking from her nap upstairs. As she rose to fetch her, she came to a decision. Yes, she would suggest it to Mr. Corrigan after dinner.

**Corrigan Department Store**

C.L. Corrigan was a warm, congenial man, even-tempered, with the extra girth to suggest a comfortable life. He was not terribly surprised to find an unexpected guest for supper. He knew his wife was a kind sort, always with a good word or a handout for anyone in need. C.L. made polite conversation with the young man and by the time the evening was over, was duly impressed. He trusted Minnie's judgment—and he could certainly use some help at the store.

"You're welcome to stay out in the carriage house tonight," he said to Charlie as Cook cleared the plates. "Tomorrow, you can go with me to the store and I'll put you to work." Beaming, Charlie thanked his benefactors. He would do his best to work hard and make good.

The next morning, C.L. showed Charlie around the store. The young man was amazed. The place held more products and household goods than he had ever seen in his life. He eagerly went to work at the simple tasks C.L. assigned him: sweeping the wooden walkway out front, restocking shelves and making deliveries.

Those were his duties in the beginning. As the weeks went by, however, Charlie's aptitude for marketing and sales became evident, and C.L. expanded his responsibilities. When Charlie put out stock, he often made attractive displays of the new goods in the front window. He suggested putting the more expensive items at the front of the store and the staples towards the rear so shoppers would have an opportunity to walk through the store and see all the merchandise.

Although he was hesitant to talk much at first, Charlie Scott enjoyed the customers. As time went on, he found he had no trouble helping them select merchandise. One patron in particular caught his attention. Pretty Mame Holdridge often came to the store on errands for her mother. She took her time selecting her purchases, debating over her choices and engaging Charlie in many conversations about the merits of a particular piece of fabric or new kitchen gadget. Charlie was baffled, since most ladies seem to know their mind about exactly what they wanted to purchase. Finally, C.L. had to suggest that perhaps Mame Holdridge was more interested in Charlie Scott than the price of potatoes.

C.L. watched with satisfaction as Charlie became an integral part of the dry goods business. This had given C.L. the opportunity to step back and pursue his dreams. He ran for Justice of the Peace and won. He then branched out and opened an office to sell insurance and was elected Village President. Charlie's life bloomed too—he and Mame married and started a family.

Eight years after Charlie Scott arrived in Fenton, C.L. Corrigan suggested

C. L. Corrigan—Justice of the Peace

that Charlie buy Corrigan's Department Store. Charlie was excited at the prospect of owning the store. The store became Scott & Co. and now Charlie was his own boss. He expanded the scope of merchandise and sold men's and women's clothing, millinery, carpet, and crockery in addition to dry goods, hardware, shoes and groceries. He continued C.L.'s policy of no-credit "Net Spot Cash" plan, and with catalogs and extensive advertising, Scott & Co. became the largest small-town store in Michigan!

# 20
## *Working Girl*
### 1892

Home of John & Martha Cowell. Photo courtesy of A J Phillips Historical Museum

Head down, eighteen-year-old Grace Colwell clutched her cloak closer as she rushed up Leroy Street, fighting the wind. She was in a hurry to get to her job as a milliner at Scott's Department Store. Gathering up the fabric of her long, full skirt to keep it out of the mud and slush, she passed Old Reliable Druggists, Louis H. Kahn Furnishings, the Fenton Steam Laundry, Becker's Shoes, and Sol Austin Tonsorial Parlor. The sharp December wind burned her cheeks, almost blew her hat off, and even cut through the heavy wool of her wrap.

The previous summer, Grace's mother, Martha, had strenuously objected when her daughter expressed a desire to go to work. She was adamant that it was not at all proper for a girl of her background and breeding to be working!

Martha Colwell would argue with most anyone until they just plain gave up, anyone except her mother-in-law. There she met her match. Grandma Colwell held the purse strings and always had the last word. Although not blood relatives, the two women were certainly cut from the same cloth.

Grace's parents argued while Grace perched out of sight, listening from the back stairwell. Mrs. Colwell lambasted her husband.

"What on earth were you thinking, John, telling Grace she could work at Scott's? Have you lost your mind?" she scolded, shaking her finger. Grace's father usually put on his hat and went for a walk rather than argue with his wife, but not this time. On this occasion, he stuck to his guns. What an argument that was.

"And what's the matter with her working at Scott's if she wants to?" John Colwell faced his wife head on. "Charlie Scott's a good man and Grace is certainly talented enough with a needle and thread. Your mother's seen to that."

"It's just not seemly! A girl of her station having to kowtow to any woman who walks in the store. I just won't have it!"

"Well, maybe you'll just have to. I've already talked to Charlie and given my permission. Grace will be in the millinery department, decorating custom hats. She won't be waiting on customers behind the counter. The only people she'll see will probably be your friends."

"Exactly!" Martha Colwell sputtered. "What will they think? We'll be disgraced. And what about Grace's reputation? She will certainly lose any good prospects for a husband."

Grace cringed, she could hear every word. So could everyone else in the household, and probably halfway down the block! She chuckled and shook her head at the thought of a husband. There were no prospects at this time, and she was fine with that. The conversation between her parents continued.

"Now, Martha, Grace is a good girl and has done us proud. Her reputation will be fine. What's she going to do around here except get in your way? You've got this house running like a top."

Martha began to speak, but her husband cut her off. "You're not to give Grace a hard time about this. She's of age and I admire her spirit. Besides, despite what you may think, I am still the head of this household. I've made up my mind."

The lady of the house bit her lip, frowned, and stormed off into the kitchen.

John Colwell sank into his leather chair and took his tobacco from his coat pocket. As he filled his pipe, he reflected that Grace was probably more like him than his wife would care to admit. He had worked since he was twelve, helping his father make bricks to build houses and commercial buildings. They had fired every single brick in the lovely three-story house where he and his family lived now.

Martha was strong-willed, but John knew better in this matter. Their daughter needed something to do, an outlet for her energy and talents. Scott & Co. seemed like a good fit.

Grace loved all types of handwork: lacemaking, embroidering, tucking and feather stitching. Needlework fed her imagination. Starting with just a bolt of nainsook and a spool of thread, she could create charming nighties and slips. Children's clothes were her specialty. Currently, she was working on a large crocheted tablecloth to be added to her hope chest, which was already half-filled with doilies and undergarments. Now she would be learning millinery.

Grace was lucky to have both her grandmothers in her life. Grandma Colwell, strong willed and opinionated, lived right in town above the Opera House. And Grandma Collins had lived with them for as long as Grace could remember. She was the one who had taught Grace to sew. Grandma Collins was best known for her beautiful hand-sewn quilts and Grace loved to watch her piece them. Surprisingly, Grandma was one of the first in Fenton to purchase a sewing machine. It was a Wilcox and Gibbs and it sat proudly in the dining room by the window. It was a graceful machine with its gleaming black metal head and flywheel atop the sturdy wooden stand and treadle. Grandmother and granddaughter marveled at the neat, even "hand stitches" they were able to so quickly produce. Grace spent many happy hours at her grandmother's side, learning everything she could.

Almost at the store, Grace brushed a stray lock of hair from her cold-reddened face. *My skin will probably be blotchy all day,* she said to herself. *Oh, so what? It doesn't matter how I look when I'm in the back at my worktable.*

Grace knew she was not a beauty, but she carried herself well and had been told that her figure was a dressmaker's dream. Even so, she had gone through high school without a beau. It bothered her more than she cared to admit.

During high school days, Grace's girlfriends often invited her to go to the post office in the evenings to wait for the mail delivery. The ritual had become a social gathering. The girls' mothers waited for the latest copy of Ladies Home Journal or Good Housekeeping. Families gathered, anxious for word from husbands, brothers and uncles who had gone off to California or Alaska in search of their fortunes. Grace's Uncle Daniel was in Alaska, and Aunt Anna was almost frantic, desperate for word from him.

The girls gossiped and giggled as they waited, hoping some of the boys from school might show up. But after a few evenings of the same talk, Grace became bored. She decided she would rather spend the time sewing with Grandma or practicing her music. As part of her proper education, she had studied piano. For some reason, her mother thought it was not ladylike to study the violin. Being ladylike was very important to Martha. It was important to Grace, too.

After learning trombone as well, Grace joined the Fenton Ladies Band. She had a lot of fun with the ladies and enjoyed marching in parades, especially when they were invited to perform in Dallas. Grace loved the band uniforms. They had been made especially for the state band competition: cadet blue jackets with gold trim, straight skirts and poke hats. She happily sewed on loose buttons or mended hems whenever asked.

Reaching her destination at last, she pulled open the door to the millinery department of Scott & Co., glad to be out of the cold wind.

"Anna, hi! Sorry I'm late," she said breathlessly, removing her cape and hat.

Her friend looked up from her work and with a small shake of her head nodded toward the far side of the room. Grace followed her gaze and saw a young man, thin and handsome. She was a bit surprised. It was unusual to see a man in the hat department.

Since the young man was busily writing on a pad of paper, Grace studied him further. He had a straight nose and deep blue eyes. His hair was parted on the side and neatly combed back. Fashionably dressed, he wore a frock coat and vest, with a bow tie and starched stand-up collar. For some reason, his serious manner struck Grace as amusing.

"Hello," she said with a causal flip of a glove. "You're the new milliner, I presume?"

Taken aback, the young man looked up from his writing, his cheeks coloring slightly.

Anna spoke up before he could answer. "This is Everett Scott, Mr. Scott's younger brother. He's here to help take inventory before he returns to law school after the holidays. Mr. Scott, this is Grace Colwell. She makes beautiful hats but terrible jokes."

Everett Scott took stock of the young woman. Not a beauty in the traditional sense, with her nose a bit large and eyes rather deep set, Grace nevertheless had a pleasant face and a sweet smile. Her long, wavy hair was unpretentiously pulled back at the nape of her neck. Most strikingly, she displayed an attractive confidence. Everett liked that.

"Oh, not a joke at all," he smiled. "I should like nothing better than to learn the fine art of attaching birds and feathers and ribbons to boiled wool." He glanced around, taking in the many spools of ribbons and bric-à-brac, all waiting to be inventoried. "There's certainly enough frippery here to go around!"

Grace frowned slightly. Was he making sport of her work? Of her? Her polite smile vanished. "I'm sure millinery wouldn't be nearly as exciting as lawyer's briefs and contract language." Critically, she looked Everett up and down. "Besides, I'm not sure you have the necessary panache to satisfy our customers. They're a rather demanding lot."

"It does sound like highly skilled work," Everett admitted. He was enjoying this exchange. Grace was different, not giggly and coy like so many of the girls he'd met in Detroit. "Perhaps you'll teach me, Miss Colwell," he finished, still smiling.

Over the next several days, Everett Scott found that recording the inventory in the millinery department took longer than expected. Conversations with Grace distracted him from counting boxes of thread and drawers of trimmings.

Everett was usually all business. He was so driven to complete his studies that he made no time for parties, dances or fairs. While studying law in Detroit, Everett lived with his mother's cousins, the Vernors. When they entertained, he made a polite show and then retired to study. But now, getting to know Grace, the possibility of being more social seemed appealing.

For her part, Grace didn't let Everett's attention distract her from her work. There was too much to do as December flew by. She and Anna busily finished hats for the Christmas season. The Ladies Band performed. Holiday preparations were underway at home on High Street. Even so, Grace enjoyed Everett's company at the store.

Before she met Everett, Grace had never thought about her boss' personal life. She knew Charlie Scott's wife had died from fever and he was a widower, but she did know much else. He was very private about his personal life. She was surprised to learn that his two young children, Walter and Maude, were living in Capac with their grandparents. Charlie Scott lived alone in a boardinghouse on Shiawassee. No wonder he was at the store from dawn to dusk. He had no real home to offer his brother while he was in town. *How sad,* she thought, *for Mr. Scott and Everett to spend Christmas at a boarding house.*

Grace had never known a holiday not celebrated to the fullest. Her mother and Grandma Colwell both enjoyed decorating and entertaining for every occasion and they did it up to the nines. Christmas at the house on High Street was always grand. There would be a large tree in the parlor, decorated on

Christmas Eve with candles, sweets, fruits, homemade decorations and small gifts. Grace's favorite decorations were the gilded egg cups filled with comfits and barley sugar. Shiny trays of festive bonbons and sugared almonds wrapped in colorful paper graced every table. Lush evergreen branches decorated the windows and doors.

Christmas dinner was a lavish feast: oyster soup, roast turkey breast, sirloin of beef, baked cauliflower and celery, cranberries and, of course, squash pie, mincemeat pie and plum pudding. After dinner, Christmas carols were sung around the piano.

One evening, instead of going directly home after work, Grace walked north to visit Grandma Colwell. Although Christmas would be celebrated at her parents' home on High Street, there was no question that Grandma Colwell was in charge of the festivities.

Grandpa Colwell had built the opera house many years ago, after the great Bridge Fire that destroyed so much of the town. Large enough to seat several hundred people and to accommodate plays, musicals, and vaudeville, the opera house even boasted a roller skating rink, sponsored by the Fenton Ladies Band.

Many celebrities had used the venue over the years. General Tom Thumb once held a one-night gala there. Frederick Douglass and Susan B. Anthony had spoken from the stage. Even now, in 1892, the opera house was still the center of entertainment for Fenton.

Grace climbed the steps to the third floor, where her grandparents now lived after moving from the house on High Street. Grandma Colwell was surprised to see Grace at the door.

"Good gracious child, come in. You'll catch your death!" she exclaimed, struggling to close the door against the cold. Grace greeted her grandma with a kiss on the cheek as she unwound her scarf from her neck and knocked the snow off her high-top shoes.

"What brings you out in this terrible weather, Grace?"

"A gift and a favor, Grandma," Grace set a large hatbox on the floor. "I'm coming from Scott & Co." Grace noticed her grandmother's slight frown. "I know you don't approve of me working there, but I really like making the beautiful hats. In fact, I've brought one for you to look at." Grace knelt down and lifted the lid of the hatbox. She pulled out a wool hat in a beautiful dark shade of purple. Red and gold ribbon circled the brim and pine cones and holly berries were tucked in the neat bow in the back of the hat. The effect was festive, but quite tasteful.

Phoebe Colwell looked at the hat admiringly. It was beautiful. Although she was reluctant to encourage Grace's work outside the home, she was proud of her granddaughter's skill. She knew from her friends that Grace's hats were in huge demand. Begrudgingly, Phoebe admitted to herself that Scott & Co. was lucky to have her.

Grace spoke up, as if reading her grandmother's thoughts. "Mr. Scott has been very kind to me, Grandma. And the people at the store are so nice. In fact, I just met Mr. Scott's younger brother, Everett, who's helping with inventory. He goes to law school in Detroit. I hear he stays with family there, the Vernors." The Vernors name certainly piqued Phoebe's interest. Everyone knew the rags to riches tale of Vernors' family and Vernors' Ginger Ale.

Grandma Colwell smiled. "All right, dear. What is the favor you want to ask?"

"Mr. Scott and Everett are living in a rooming house," explained Grace. "You might remember that Mr. Scott's wife died several years ago. He sold their house here in town and sent his two little children to Capac to live with his parents. Now he spends all his time at the store. I think it's such a shame, especially at Christmas. I can't even imagine spending the holidays in a lonely boarding house."

Phoebe listened intently, watching her granddaughter's face as she spoke. "Oh, I see," was all she said.

Grace continued, speaking more intently. "Grandma, I'd like you to invite Everett and Mr. Scott to Christmas dinner. They might not have any other place to go. It doesn't seem right." Grace waited to hear what her grandmother would say.

Highly aware of the politics in Fenton's business community, the older woman paused to consider this request. Scott & Co. was a prominent concern and Charlie Scott was certainly an up-and-comer. Everett sounded like he had prospects, too. And this was the first time Grace had shown much interest in a young man. Yes, it might be a good idea to include the Scotts in their Christmas festivities.

Grace scanned her grandmother's face and quickly added, "Everett is very interested in politics. I told him Grandpa had been a delegate to the Democratic convention. He would love to talk to him. Grandpa would enjoy it, too."

Phoebe smiled at her granddaughter and came straight to the point. "So you like this young man? Everett?"

Grace blushed and nodded.

The Scotts were a welcome addition to the Colwell's celebration and helped make Christmas a big success. Charlie Scott presented Phoebe and Martha with fine kid leather gloves from New York. He asked Grandpa Colwell, known as DG, about the recent renovations to the Opera House. The old gentleman was happy to describe the new stage, dressing rooms and improved seating. He invited Charlie to tour it some time.

Charlie Scott excitedly talked of the upcoming World's Columbian Exposition in Chicago. He hoped to visit the exposition and Marshall Field's Department Store, which he had heard so much about. Everett was a bit more reserved in conversation but, after some cajoling from his brother, regaled the group with tales from his law studies and life in Detroit with the Vernors family.

After the Christmas festivities, the New Year brought another round of socializing. Traditionally, New Year's Day was for visiting. Ladies stayed home to receive visitors; the gentlemen made the calls. At the house on High Street, Grace finished setting out the trays and stood back, admiring the spread. A handsomely ornamented cake stood high on a silver stand in the center of the table, surrounded by vases of deep red poinsettias and fragrant evergreen branches. Phoebe, Martha and Grace had decorated lemon tea cakes and butter

Fenton Ladies' Cornet Band. Photo courtesy of A J Phillips Historical Museum

biscuits, stamping them with raised patterned wooden blocks. There were plat-
ters of tea sandwiches of tongue, ham and potted veal along with pickled oys-
ters, sardines and cold salads. Martha had taken a suggestion from Jennie June's
"American Cookery Book" and had arranged a dish of oranges decorated with
tufts of green moss and sprigs of scarlet geranium.

Fortunately, the day had dawned sunny. The house was ready for callers and
it would have been a shame for bad weather to dampen the occasion. Some
years, the Colwell ladies entertained as many as fifty visitors, most of them
business associates of the Colwell men. They were prepared for at least that
many on this day.

Grace served drinks, a proper duty for the daughter of the house. She spent
the day greeting callers politely, making light conversation as she offered them
claret punch, cider or tea.

Late in the afternoon, as the flow of guests began to wane, she was pleased
to see Everett, who had come alone. Charlie was otherwise engaged. Everett
accepted Grace's offer of tea and they chatted.

"Most of my work at the department store is in the back office," he said.
"Charlie would be talking to everyone, but I know very few of the gentlemen
here."

"Let me introduce you," offered Grace. She took him by the elbow and whispered, "If you're going to have a law practice, you need to make connections."

# 21
## *Everett Returns Home*

1896

Everett Scott being admitted to the Bar

---

Charlie paced the train platform, checked his pocket watch once again and stuffed it back in his vest pocket, awaiting the arrival of the 12:05 from Detroit. It would be good have Everett back in town permanently. It was a warm spring day and the crabapple trees had budded out almost overnight. The sun shone brightly. He glanced up when he heard a well-dressed gentleman call out.

"Why, Mr. Scott! Fancy running into you here." The gentleman held out his hand to shake Charlie's. "You might not remember me, Horace Rackham."

Charlie knew Mr. Rackham, but not well. His wife, Mary Horton, had grown up in Fenton. She was good friends with Charlie's new partners, Margaret and Frederick Rolland.

"It's nice to see you, Mr. Rackham. I haven't noticed you around much lately."

"No, I sold the farm outside of town a few years ago. We're back in Detroit now. I'm practicing law again. And how about you? Still spending all your time at the department store? I stopped in while I was in town. Most impressive!"

With over forty employees, Scott & Co was now the town's largest retail establishment, but Charlie was always looking for improvements. After a recent renovation, the two-story building stretched across four storefronts on Leroy and Third.

"Just trying to keep up with the times," said Charlie, his pride evident. "From what I hear, Hudson's department store in Detroit and even Marshall Field's in Chicago are pretty stiff competition. Just incredible, the services they're offering: tearooms, lavatories, elevators." He shook his head in amazement. "So, Mr. Rackham, what brings you here?"

"I'm catching the train back to Detroit. Had to come into town to see a friend of yours, Judge Corrigan, about the new fire hall. Are you headed to Detroit, too?"

"Not today. My brother Everett is coming back to Fenton to settle down. Maybe you know him. He's been practicing law at Stillwagoner & Fleming."

"No, can't say I do. But I'm surprised that he's moving here. Most young attorneys want to be where all the action is. Not too many are fans of small towns like I am. I love small towns and their people. They talk my language. But I suppose I'm part of a rare breed."

Charlie chuckled. "I'll be glad to have Everett back, that's certain. The move is understandable if you know the details. It might have something to do with a certain young lady in my millinery department."

# 22
## Matchmaking

1900

Charlie and Everett had gone up to their parents' farm in Capac to visit Charlie's children, Maude and Walter. It was a pleasant afternoon, sitting under the shade trees in the front yard. Grandpa Floyd entertained Walter with a game of horseshoes. Maude sipped lemonade and listened to Charlie and Everett talk. The brothers were glad it was Sunday. Otherwise, their father would have put them to work.

"So, Charlie," their ma said half-kiddingly. "We know Everett's fixin' to get himself married one of these days. How about you? You ever think of getting married again?" She looked lovingly at her grandchildren, Walter and Maude. They had been a joy to raise these past several years, but would be entering high school soon, and she and her husband were getting older.

Charlie looked up, surprised. He hadn't considered remarriage. How could any woman hold a candle to his first wife, Mary Holdridge? When he had come to Fenton and begun working at the store, Mary—called Mame by her friends—often came in on errands for her mother, dawdling until Charlie was free to help her with her shopping. At first he couldn't believe she might be sweet on him until Mr. Corrigan pointed it out one day.

With his stammer and his poor background, Charlie didn't think he had much to offer Mary. But she persisted and, as the saying goes, she chased him until he caught her!

Their marriage was a good one and Charlie considered himself lucky to have such a quiet and sweet wife. They were even happier when their two children, Walter and Maude, arrived. Then the fever took Mary. Charlie was devastated. Mary's own mother had died just a year before. Who would look after the babies? Charlie turned to his parents up in Capac, who agreed to take the children in for as long as Charlie needed. Looking back Charlie reflected on the many changes in his circumstances. Over the years working with the public in the dry goods store he'd gradually lost his stutter. He was a confident successful businessman now and certainly he had much more to offer now than when he courted his first wife.

Maude's ears perked up. "If you got married again, Walter and I could come back and live with you in Fenton. I could go to high school there."

"You'd like that?" he asked her.

"Oh Father, that would be wonderful."

Charlie looked at Maude and suddenly realized how much time had slipped away. She was becoming a beautiful young woman. The farm here in Capac was really no place for a young girl entering high school. Before he knew it, his little girl would be married herself, and Walter would be grown too.

Living in the boardinghouse, it had been easy for Charlie to put all his time and energy into working at the store. He admitted to himself that he was lonely. It would be nice to have a real home and be together again as a family.

Walter had been listening to the conversation as well. "Will you do it, Father?" he asked.

Charlie wasn't sure. He laughed the question off. "What makes you think you'd like my new wife? If I *were* to remarry, that is. She could be mean and ugly and horrid."

Maude shook her head, sausage curls bouncing. "Choose Miss Rolland! She's pretty and she's ever so nice."

Charlie paused to think. Helen Rolland was a good- looker, all right. She was the sister of his friend Frederick Rolland. Although she was quite a bit younger than Charlie, she seemed to have a good head on her shoulders. As far as he knew she was unattached.

"We'll see," Charlie said to his children. He kept the rest of his thoughts to himself.

*Maude came up with a good idea. I just might call on Helen this week.*

# 23
## Marshall Fields Department Store

CHICAGO—JUNE 1901

The wedding was a quiet affair. Helen wanted to have it at her brother Frederick's home in Lake View, Chicago. Charlie was amenable. He wanted to please Helen. After all, she was taking on a ready-made family. Besides, he was more than happy for an excuse to go to Chicago and visit Marshall Field & Co., the store he had heard so much about. It was said to be the largest department store in the country.

The day after the wedding, Fred and his wife Margaret took Charlie and Helen downtown by carriage. From there they caught a ride on the new trolley car system.

The trolley bell clanged as the car stopped just under the iconic brass clock jutting out over the Marshall Field entrance at State and Washington Streets. Chicago weather had given the brass clock a green patina. The store was a sight to behold. It ran the length of the entire block and rose up eight stories. Large glass display windows stretched the entire length of the building. Four enormous granite pillars flanked the grand entrance. Charlie and Helen had never seen anything like this.

"Its no accident this trolley stops right in

Advertisements for Scott & Co. Photos courtesy of A J Phillips Historical Museum

front of the entrance to Marshall Field & Co.," Fred remarked. "When Mr. Field invested in the trolley system it was his idea to have it run in a loop through downtown Chicago with a stop right in front of his store."

"Pretty brilliant," Charlie replied. "Too bad Fenton isn't big enough for a trolley."

The doorman in his green and gold uniform stood outside the entrance. Two glass doors gleamed and flanked three circular doors that were most unusual. Margaret and Charlie stood and watched the revolving circular glass doors. Shoppers entered and walked in a half circle and then exited smoothly into the main lobby.

"It's easy," Fred laughed. He walked up to the door and let Margaret enter first, gathering her large skirt close. Fred entered and then hesitantly Helen and Charlie followed.

Inside, Charlie noticed immediately that the store was lit with electric lights, not gas. To their right, a clerk in a black dress ran a check room for coats and packages.

"Charlie, look at everything offered here," Helen pointed to a large sign that listed the variety of services offered. "Glove and garment repair, jewelry repair, a cobbler, a post office, and even a nursery for young children. They offer theater tickets and travel arrangements. You would never need to shop anywhere else," she marveled. Charlie nodded in agreement.

They walked onto the sales floor.

"Oh, my," was all Helen could say. There were rich mahogany counters with glass shelves and plush carpeting ran the length of the aisles. Large mirrors were stationed around the elaborate displays. The first floor held perfumes and jewelry. Helen and Margaret walked ahead admiring the broaches, necklaces, earrings and rings. Charlie couldn't help notice that one particular brooch caught Helen's eye. It was gold and crystal in a spray setting. He made a note to try to purchase it when she wasn't looking. When they had finished browsing the jewelry department they looked for the elevators to the other floors. Instead they found a wooden moving staircase.

"Charlie, look! The stairs are moving!" Helen cried out.

"It's called an escalator," Fred said. "And no wonder you've never seen one. It was just invented last year and Marshall Fields is one of the first places to install it. There are elevators, too, but the escalator is much more fun."

"Well I'm certainly going to try this escalator," Helen said and gingerly stepped onto the moving stairway and held tight to the handrail. The next floor held the ladies' department.

"Oh, Margaret, look at this." Helen held up a white silk beaded reticule. "I should have shopped here for my wedding outfit and trousseau. How beautiful."

They ooh-ed and ahh-ed over Alexandre kid gloves, Chantilly lace parasols, folding silk fans with gold handles, and silk beaded satchels.

"Oh look how pretty this is," Margaret held up a tortoiseshell hair comb. "It would look beautiful in your auburn hair. You must get it."

They continued exploring the huge department store floor by floor. In the men's department they found collars, suspenders, smoking capes and bumble shoots. One floor was completely filled with children's clothing and another had household goods, including Persian rugs and fine china.

On the seventh floor was the tea room called the Walnut Room. Margaret suggested they rest and have lunch.

"You simply must try the chicken pot pie," she said. "It's what Marshall Field's is best known for and there's the funniest story about the origins of the pot pie and the tea room." They looked up from their menus expectantly.

"Mrs. Herring was a clerk in the ladies' department. She noticed her customers would become weary at lunch time and once even shared her own lunch with a shopper. So Mrs. Herring started making chicken pot pies at home and bringing them to the store. They became hugely popular. But when the department manager discovered he had customers sitting on boxes in a storage room eating chicken pot pie he was livid. He was going to fire her but Mr. Marshall Field got wind of it and intervened. He thought she was very enterprising and told the department manager they certainly didn't want their customers to leave the store to find something to eat. Better they stay right in the store and continue their shopping after lunch."

"Well we will certainly have to try the famous Chicken Pot Pie now that we know the story," said Fred.

Harry Selfridge was the general retail manager of the store, second only to Mr. Marshall Field himself. Charlie had hoped for an interview with Mr. Selfridge but he thought it would be impertinent to wire ahead to request a meeting. He was blessed with a stroke of luck, however, when the group decided to take an elevator car down to the ground floor after lunch. As they approached the bank of six elaborately decorated doors, Charlie spotted Mr. Selfridge waiting for an elevator.

"Mr. Selfridge," Charlie called. "I am so anxious to meet you and offer my congratulations on this fine establishment." Mr. Selfridge turned and looked at Charlie in surprise. Charlie held out his hand.

"I'm Charlie Scott. I'm visiting from Michigan. I own a modest department store there and I was so anxious to see Marshall Field's for myself. It is everything I had heard and more."

"Why thank you," Mr. Selfridge said and shook Charlie's hand. "It's a pleasure to meet you. I'm always pleased to meet a fellow businessman and I'm more than happy to brag about our store." He chuckled and continued, "We have over 500 employees: doormen, cash boys, clerks, supervisors and elevator operators. In another year, we're expanding and will add four more stories to this building." He turned to Margaret and Helen. "And how did you enjoy your day shopping at Marshall Field & Co.?"

They nodded excitedly. "It's quite the department store, Mr. Selfridge. I've never seen anything quite like it," said Helen.

"We're considering putting in a library on the top floor, for the ladies to relax and read a magazine," Mr. Selfridge said. "What are your thoughts on that idea? I would certainly appreciate a ladies' perspective."

"Oh what a wonderful idea," said Margaret. "A quiet, smoke-free ladies' lounge and library sounded quite pleasant, especially after a long day of exploring the massive departments of Marshall Field's. We enjoyed lunch in the tea room. I don't know of any other place that offers such amenities."

A chime sounded as one of the elevator cars arrived at their floor. Mr. Selfridge stepped in and said goodbye. "I'm going up to the executive offices. There will be another car along shortly to take you downstairs."

When the next car arrived, the elevator attendant opened the brass grate and slid open the glass doors for the four to step in. He firmly closed the grate and then slid the door shut, pushed a lever—and down they dropped. Watching the floors fly past was a strange and exhilarating experience for Charlie and Helen. When the car stopped at ground level, the couple from Fenton was more than a little relieved.

# 24
## The Dream Victorian

### 1896—1902

Home of Everett & Grace Scott. Photo courtesy of A J Phillips Historical Museum

It was a lengthy courtship. Everett had been adamant that his law practice be firmly established before he took on the responsibilities of married life. Although he had completed his law studies early, he had to wait until he turned twenty-one to take the bar exam. After that, he spent two years working for a law firm in Detroit. All this time he and Grace courted, looking forward to the time when they would be married.

There were excursions to Woodhull's Landing to hear concerts, and baseball games at the town ball field. Once, the Boston Bloomer Girls team came to play in Fenton. Some evenings were spent at the Opera House to see the latest touring play or, on one occasion, Thomas Edison's new "Animatiscope" movie.

Grace's favorite pastime, however, was simply a leisurely stroll with Everett around the newly completed Water Works Park and through the streets of the village. She especially loved looking at the beautiful homes along Shiawassee Avenue. A.J. Phillips' home was the most imposing: three stories tall with a porch across the entire front, metal relief work over the front door and etched glass. His son Winfield Phillips' house was also grand, and ground had been broken for Harry Phillips' new house. But the one that really caught Grace's eye was a lovely older Victorian. She called it her dream home. Often they would walk past it in the evening after supper, Grace's hand tucked in the crook of Everett's elbow.

The house had been built in 1880 by Josiah Buckbee, a businessman and banker. It boasted a double front glassed door, a huge side porch and a large carriage house in the rear. The foundation was high with large windows, indicating a roomy cellar. The current owner was Mr. Damon, who traveled the Wild West shows as a sharpshooter.

"Oh, Everett, look at that turret! Isn't it charming? And the bay windows with the arched peaks and all the trim!" Grace exclaimed, longing in her voice.

Everett smiled. He admired the house, too. Realizing how difficult it had been for Grace to wait for him to be established, he promised his patient fiancée that one day it would be hers.

# 25
# A Moral Dilemma

1903

After Emma Gould departed, Everett waited what he felt was a respectable amount of time before donning his bowler hat and Inverness coat and heading down the dark narrow stairs from his law office. The wind whipped his face as he opened the door to the street. He hurried towards Scott & Co., hoping Charlie would be in his office. What a sticky wicket this was! He needed to talk to his older brother about it. Reaching the store, Everett strode across the busy sales floor and bounded up the back stairs.

Charlie looked up from his desk and greeted his brother cheerfully. "Everett! Good to see you. Out wedding shopping?"

Everett shook his head. "No. Not today. Listen, do you suppose we could talk for a minute? It's rather urgent."

Charlie took a quick look around to see if any of his employees might have overheard. Everett fidgeted with his waistcoat and nervously glanced overhead at the cash and receipt boxes which ran on wires from the sales floor up to the cash office and back again. They moved constantly. Business at the large, newly renovated store was good.

"Shut the door so we can talk," said Charlie. "Is Grace all right? Has something happened?"

"No, no, Grace is fine. She's busy getting ready for the wedding. She tells me there's a lot to do. And you know her mother. If Grace wasn't busy enough, Martha would create something. No, this is business."

"Now you've got me worried. Should I be?"

Everett took a deep breath and continued. "Emma Gould just came to see me. You remember her? She was Judson Phillips' widow. She's married to Hadley Gould, now. He's Dr. Gould's brother. It seems the Phillips' family attorney is out of town and she needed a legal opinion. She said she came to me because I'm the new guy in town."

"What about?"

"It's a cockamamie story. She's gotten the idea that Win Phillips has cheated her out of money. She thinks Win renewed the patents Judson held but put them in his own name. She wants me to look into it."

"What do you think of it all?" asked Charlie.

"It seems to me that the Phillips have done right by Emma since Judson passed away," answered Everett with a shake of his head. "They've been wonderful to her. She's still living comfortably in the house and Julia Phillips sees to it when she or the children need something. But Emma thinks she's been swindled. I don't know what to think."

"That is certainly hard to believe, in my opinion. What did you tell Emma?"

"I told her I'd have to think about it. This could be a real mess if I go digging around inferring that Win and the Phillips have cheated their own sister-in-law."

Everett stood and paced, then continued. "Whether it's true or not, there's no good outcome for me. I certainly don't want to get in the middle of a powerful family's squabble. If I offend the Phillips, who would have the nerve to use me as their attorney after that?" He stopped and laid both hands on Charlie's desk. "This could affect you, too."

"Me? What does this have to do with me?"

"Charlie, think about it. If the Phillips blackball Everett Scott, they'll likely boycott Scott & Co. as well. And if the Phillips ladies quit shopping here, don't you think their Bay Club friends won't follow suit? Your store is the best in town, but that might be all they need to take their business elsewhere. The department stores in Detroit are only two hours away by train."

Charlie sat thoughtfully, mulling over Everett's words. Now he could see how this could have disastrous consequences for both of them. It wouldn't necessarily go well for Emma Gould either. If Everett proved that her brother-in-law had cheated her, how would that look? All their reputations would suffer. Charlie silently filled his pipe and glanced again at his brother, who had slumped back in a chair.

Everett had learned a great deal about the ways of the world while he was in law school in Detroit. Now in Fenton, working hard to establish his law practice, he had made all the right moves: he had a fine office on Leroy, had joined the Masons and the Maccabees, he was a member of the Democratic Party. He even had his eye on the governorship or the State Supreme Court. But for all his ambition, Everett was a very ethical man. He went into law because he believed in doing what was right. Now he was discovering that it wasn't always easy to know what to do. This was going to be a difficult decision.

# 26

## Fenton Mourns

The train horn blew mournfully. Grace sat ramrod straight, clutching her handbag, her body jostled by the rhythmic motion of the train over the tracks. She closed her eyes tight in an attempt to shut out the world around her. Her brothers-in-law, Charlie and Floyd, sat with her in the train compartment along with Reverend Work. The men talked quietly amongst themselves. Anxious to be back home, safe in her own house with her children, Grace did her best to tune the voices out. She tried to make her mind a blank, but the events of the last week played over and over in her head, surreal and horrible.

It began one evening when Everett had come home from the office early, complaining of pain in his abdomen. He excused himself from dinner to retire. Grace gave him a tonic, but the next day the pain was so severe she called Dr. Gould. He diagnosed Everett with appendicitis. They despaired for his health for the next few days until he improved enough to travel and Dr. Gould recommended they go to Harper Hospital in Detroit for surgery.

Arrangements were hurriedly made. As they prepared for the trip, Everett was able to take some weak tea and toast on a bed tray. He asked two-year-old Billie to join him. Despite Everett's pain, they chatted happily. Grace blinked back tears as she watched her husband and son. She hoped Billie would remember the moment.

Everett endured the two-hour trip to the hospital and was rushed into surgery. The doctor came out to speak to the family after the operation. His voice was gentle, but serious.

"I'm afraid the surgery revealed intestinal adhesions. The disease has reached a chronic stage. We'll just have to wait and see." His tone was not hopeful.

Grace hurried in to see Everett, lying so still and gray on the hospital bed. *Only five years! They had courted longer than that, such a short time as husband and wife.* Grace knew she should be grateful for the good times and not despair over the future that could have been, but it was heartbreaking. She recalled the boat trip through the Thousand Islands in Quebec they had taken with

Harry and Georgia Phillips two years previously. Grace hadn't wanted to travel so soon after Billie was born, but Everett had insisted. Now she was glad they had gone.

Grace sat in a chair at the head of the narrow hospital bed. Charlie handed her Everett's bible, well-worn with many notes in the margin. She read aloud from it, not knowing if her husband could hear, but still deriving comfort from the words. "The Lord is my Shepherd, I shall not want..."

A few hours later, Everett's breathing became shallow and labored. The doctor was quickly summoned. After a short examination, he laid Everett's pale hand on the coverlet. "He's gone," the doctor whispered.

The slowing of the train and a long whistle blast brought Grace back to the present. They had arrived home to Fenton. Opening her eyes, she was surprised by the sight of black drapes hanging over the depot windows and throngs of people packing the platform. News of Everett's death had been wired ahead, and much of the town had turned out—men, women and even children. Grace was touched to see the crowd, somber as it was.

Memories flooded Grace's mind again. Everett had been wonderful with children. She could tell while they courted that he would be a fine father by the way he doted on Maude, his favorite niece. Later, with his own children, Everett was even more patient and loving. Helen would hide behind the front door, leaping out to surprise him when he returned home at night. Without fail, Everett always acted surprised. He even allowed the children in his office, letting them play under his desk while he worked. How Helen and Billie would miss him!

The clanging of the bell announced the train had stopped. Charlie assisted her as they alighted and walked down to the baggage car, the crowd was respectfully silent. The hearse was already waiting for Everett's casket to be unloaded. Now the sad business of planning his funeral would begin.

Everett's body was laid out in the parlor at the much-loved Victorian home. Grace thought it best to keep Billie and Helen out of the room, but Helen was strong-willed, even at four years of age. That evening, after most of the mourners had left and Grace was in the kitchen, she heard Helen scream. The child had snuck into the parlor and saw her father in his half-closed casket. Helen thought his legs had been cut off! Grace picked the little child up and held her tightly and rocked her as they both cried.

The service was held at 10:30 Saturday morning. Immediate family and close friends crowded inside the parlor and front room as Reverend Work conducted the prayer service. Ashley Phillips, the village president, had issued a proclamation in the Fenton Independent that all businesses were to be closed during the funeral. Townsfolk gathered in front of the house and along Shiawassee Avenue for half the block. The sheer size of the crowd stirred Grace's heart. It was overwhelming to see how many lives Everett had touched.

After the service, the wooden casket was carried out to the hearse. The sun shone on the brightly colored autumn leaves, but the crisp wind of late October foretold the coming winter. The two black mares hitched to the wagon were not used to such a large crowd. They whinnied nervously, shook their heads and pawed the dirt as the funeral procession began.

Grace, Helen and Billie walked behind the hearse with Everett's brother Charlie and his wife Helen. Everett's other brothers and sisters walked, too. Fred, Florence and Pearle had come all the way from Colorado. The Knights Templar marched behind them in formation, in their black dress uniforms and hats with the big white plumes. Behind them, the Fenton Village Band played dirges. The crowd followed, and it seemed as if the entire town walked up the hill to Oakwood Cemetery to pay their last respects.

Over the next few weeks, Grace pondered her options. Everett had been a very prudent man. Goodness knows, she had waited eight years so that when they married he was well-established in his law practice and had a paid-for house to offer her. *He planned for every contingency except this,* she thought ruefully.

Now she needed to find a way to support her family. Grace knew Charlie would be happy to have her back in the millinery department at Scott & Co. Her parents wanted her to move back with them. Neither option appealed to her. She thought long and hard, trying to imagine what Everett would have wanted her to do. He always admired her resourcefulness and independence. Grace didn't want to let him down now. Finally, a solution came to mind. She invited the family to tea to inform them of her plans, hoping everyone would be amenable.

She looked around the room and summoned her courage.

"I want to thank everyone for all the help you've given us these last few weeks," she began. "It's been such a shock. Everett was a wonderful husband, father, and brother. And now that he's gone, I know we all want what's best for Helen and Billie." Uncertain, Grace paused for a moment and looked around. Charlie gave her an encouraging nod. She had talked to him and Helen earlier and knew she had their support.

She resumed her speech. "Everett and I loved this house. I don't want to leave it and I want to be here for the children. So," Grace took a deep breath. "I've decided to take in boarders."

The room was still. "I'll have to have some renovations done, and I'm thinking I'll have the carriage house converted so the children and I can live there," she continued, speaking hurriedly. "It's going to take some time, but I've talked to Reverend Work and he has given me his blessing. In fact, he expressed interest in renting a room when the house is ready."

Grace's mother sat rigidly on the divan, tight-lipped. Grace knew she would not approve, but she pressed on.

"I've asked Charlie and Helen to keep little Helen for a few months while the renovations are completed. And Mother, I'm wondering if Billie could

stay with you and Father." Grace had already broached the subject with her father. He was only too happy to agree. Billie needed a man's influence, after all. He assured his daughter that they would overcome her mother's objections.

The Carriage House. Photo courtesy of
A J Phillips Historical Museum

# 27
## Staying with Grandma and Grandpa
### 1909

Little Billie often spent time with Grandma and Grandpa Colwell, his mother's parents. In the winter, they stayed in town at the Colwell's brick house on High Street. Billie loved playing there. The house was four stories tall, including the cupola. Looking out from that lofty perch, Billie could see the entire village of Fenton. On a clear day, he could see over the five lakes toward Flint. A circular staircase ran up all four stories. This often led to mischief. Billie ran up and down the stairs and threw things down from the cupola at the top. Often, when he heard his grandmother calling him to get up in the morning, he would pull off his blanket and throw it down the side of the stairs, hoping it would envelop her.

In the summer, Grandma and Grandpa Colwell stayed at their farmhouse a mile out of town. The house sat back from the road in a stand of beautiful maple trees. Nearby, there was a tool shed and several small outbuildings. Further back were two large barns, several silos, a large machine shed and a corn crib. John Colwell worked a couple hundred acres with the usual horses, cows, pigs and occasionally sheep, also raising food for the livestock. He was not the most dedicated of farmers, but did well enough to make a fair living.

Having begun brickmaking with his father at age twelve, Grandpa Colwell thought a boy was never too young for responsibility. He spent a lot of time with Billie, instilling in the boy his belief in the value of hard work.

"See these bricks?" grandpa said to Billie and rubbed his hands along the surface. "My father and I made every single brick for this house on High Street. I wasn't much older than you."

"Really?" Billie was amazed. Grandpa's hands were big and strong and weathered. Billie reached up to touch the bricks and felt how rough and coarse they were. The house was huge. He wondered just how many bricks there were and how long it had taken his grandpa to make all those bricks. *Grandpa can do just about anything,* he thought. *I want to be like grandpa.*

So Billie worked hard. He learned to fetch wood from the woodshed to fuel the kitchen range. This was a very important job. That fire had to be kept going at all times to heat the water in the tank, keep the chicken food simmering and cook the kettle of soup. Billie had chores during the winter at the High Street house, too. The coal scuttles had to be kept full. In the sitting room was the "base burner," which had a tea kettle on top to keep the room warm and humid. In the evenings, Grandpa Colwell would sit by the base burner and kick off his shoes to warm his feet on the iron frame around the glass door. Billie tried to put his feet up there, too, but he was not quite big enough. His grandma sat in front of the east window, a little further from the stove, usually sewing.

In the winter, Billie went back and forth to the farm with his grandpa, either by horse and buggy, a team and wagon, or a two-horse sleigh. He loved riding high up on top of the load. On one trip they were hauling cornstalks from the field to feed the cattle for the winter. As Grandpa Colwell turned the wagon to bring it next to the silo, the team cut the corner too sharply. Over went the load, Billie and all, burying the boy in the pile of cornstalks. At first Billie thought it was great fun being buried in all those cornstalks, until he felt a sharp cut on his face and cried out. Grandpa hopped down from the wagon seat and dug frantically through the cornstalks trying to find him. He felt the sharp prongs of a pitchfork and pulled it out and tossed it to the side.

"Billie! Billie!" he called. He pulled Billie out of the heap of cornstalks and as he brushed away the stalks from Billie's plaid jacket he saw that his grandson's face was covered in blood!

"Hold still," he commanded sharply. He pulled the neckerchief off his own neck and tied it tightly around Billie's head, the cut was dangerously close to the boy's eye. "Its alright, Billie. Doc will get you fixed up." Grandpa's voice was shaky.

He held Billie tightly as he swung back onto the wagon.

"Giddyup, yup!" Grandpa hollered at the horses. Billie could feel grandpa's strong grip around his waist and he could hear the crack of the whip, but he couldn't see a thing. Grandpa whipped the team to go faster and faster. The wagon bounced and jolted precariously over the ruts in the road. Billie had never known Grandpa to drive this fast before.

Once in town Dr. Ingram examined the cut.

"It was certainly a small miracle that you didn't lose your eye," Dr. Ingram said. Billie flinched as the doctor cleaned the wound and then applied

Mercurochrome. It stung badly but Billie couldn't let Grandpa see him cry.

"But Grandpa," Billie complained, "I didn't get to see you race the horses. Can we do it again?"

Of all the animals on the farm the lambs were Billie's favorite. He loved to watch them hop about playing and chasing each other. The tiny bleats made him laugh.

One fall day, Grandpa had Billie help him gather the sheep from the fields and herd them down the lane to the barn on the south farm. They walked together without talking. Billie dragged a long stick in the dirt as they walked. Then without warning Grandpa grabbed a lamb and, quick as lightning, cut its tail off with a knife! Billie was shocked.

"Grandpa! What are you doing?" He'd never known his grandpa to hurt an animal before and he was shocked. Grandpa turned and gently squeezed Billie's shoulder.

"Look," he said and showed him the little tail. "This tail is all full of thistles and dirt. If I'd left this tail on that little fella would have been in constant pain. He could have gotten an infection and died. But look at him now. He's just fine." He then pointed to the lamb, already frolicking again.

Sometimes in late fall the weather turned cold before Grandma and Grandpa returned to the house in town. When Billie stayed with them and it was too chilly to sleep upstairs, Grandma Colwell made a cozy bed for Billie by tying the dining room chairs together and laying a feather bed on top of the chairs. Billie loved to lay there in his makeshift bed, next to the stove, warm and cozy.

# 28
## Halley's Comet

MAY 1910

Colwell Opera House. Photo courtesy of A J Phillips Historical Museum

Stories about Halley's Comet were in the newspaper every day. There were ominous predictions of catastrophe: the comet's tail contained poisonous gas that would wipe out life on Earth as it passed through the atmosphere; the comet would be closer than ever before and might collide with Earth. Mark Twain had been born during Halley's Comet in 1835 and he predicted his own death as it passed by again. Sales of telescopes soared.

Earlier in the year, another comet had flashed through the sky, totally unpredicted and visible to the naked eye. Dubbed the Daylight Comet, it only served to stir up speculation and excitement for Halley's Comet in the spring.

Grace thought it was all hogwash—but it was a great excuse for a party.

She and Everett always loved to entertain but, after his death two years ago, her heart just hadn't been in it. Somehow, this excitement seemed like a good opportunity so shake off her mourning and begin again. The rooftop of the Opera House would be the perfect spot for her Halley's Comet party.

Grace's mother was the ultimate party planner. Together they designed the menu and the decorations, deciding, of course, on a celestial theme. The guest list included Charlie and Helen Scott, Charlie's daughter Maude, Floyd Scott, the Rollands, the Eddys, the Holdridges, and the Busseys.

That evening the comet was to appear, crowds gathered on lawns, street corners and down in Water Works Park. Grace's guests huddled on the Opera House roof, drinks in hand. All eyes looked towards the heaven. As soon as it was spotted, cheers rang out. There it was, high in the sky: Halley's Comet! A great white ball of fire with a long pointed tail, it was the most memorable sight of 1910.

# 29
## *It Takes a Village*

1911

Rev. John & Grace McWilliams Presbyterian Manse

G race had her hands full running the boarding house and raising her two energetic children. Every morning, Helen and Billie shot out the back door, climbed over the fence and ran through the A. J. Phillips & Co. stock shed to get to North Ward School. They wanted to be on time, of course, but were also anxious to see their friends. Five-year-old Billie's best friend was little Nellie Phillips. Helen teased her brother about his sweetheart, but Billie didn't care. Nellie was his sweetheart, and he knew that someday they would get married.

Grace's family members were a wonderful help with the children. Not only did her parents spent time with Billie, but her brother-in-law and sister-in-law,

Charlie and Helen, would take little Helen to stay with them too. This gave Grace a chance to take care of the boarding house and to catch up on her chores. During the winter, their uncle Charlie took them for sleigh rides—merry bells jingling and warm soapstone heaters tucked under the buffalo robe. A few times, Charlie took them out to see their father's favorite dappled grey mare.

"I'm afraid taking Billie and Helen to see Everett's horse was not such a good idea," he told Grace when they returned home from their outing. "They miss their father so much."

Grace was silent for a moment. She missed Everett fiercely, too. "Charlie, I am so thankful for all you do for the children. I can't teach them the things a father would. They need a man in their life. Everett would be so pleased to see you look after them."

"Oh, Grace, you know I feel for them. When Mame died and I had Walter and Maude to raise by myself I didn't know how I could manage. It broke my heart to send them to stay with my parents in Capac but I didn't feel I had any other choice. I love being able to step in and help you with Billie and Helen."

The neighbors assisted as well, especially with Billie, who was quite a handful. Lawson Becker always sat three rows behind Grace and the children in church. When five-year-old Billie would get restless during the service, Mr. Becker motioned to the little boy to come and sit with him. His pockets were full of coins, keys and sometimes even a piece of candy. When church let out, Billie often rode home with the Beckers in their Packard touring car.

One day Joe Dorland asked Billie, "Do you have a coaster wagon?" Joe owned a scrap plant at the foundry and would pay boys for scrap metal. Bill nodded

"Well then, go around to your neighbors, pick up all the iron and bring it back." Joe held up a sample of what he wanted.

After trudging all over town, Billie returned with his wagon full. The foreman inspected it, weighed it, and gave Billie a dime payment! He was in business!

Helen was the more studious of the two youngsters. Grace kept her busy with deportment and music lessons as well as her regular schoolwork. She knew she was strict with her daughter, but wanted to be sure that Helen was raised to be a proper lady with all the social graces.

Grace herself loved parties, but not necessarily children's parties. Her friends teased her that she had planned for Helen and Billie to be born on the same day two years apart just so she would only have to have one birthday party a year. Grace had to smile at the absurdity, but she never once contradicted them.

In the midst of her busy life, Grace held fast to her Presbyterian faith as a comfort and refuge. In 1911, three years after Everett's death, a new minister was assigned to the church. Reverend Work had boarded at Grace's rooming house, but the new pastor, John McWilliams, chose to live in the manse. When he was introduced to the congregation, they learned that their new reverend had studied at Grove City College, Princeton Theological Seminary and McCormick Seminary in Chicago. While still a student, he built a small rural church in South Dakota. Fenton Presbyterian was his first real pastorate, and he worked hard to become a valued part of the community. The congregation quickly grew to love "Reverend Mac." Billie was impressed by the fact that he smoked cigars! Grace liked him, too.

One morning Martha Colwell stopped in to see her daughter. Grace was sewing in the front room and feeling very cheerful. So cheerful, in fact, that Martha commented on it.

"What's wrong? Why are you so happy today?" Grace did not speak but lifted up her sewing and made her mother smell it.

"Oh, no," she cried, "Not that smoker man again!"

Grace's eyes shined, "Yes, and he is going to be a part of the family."

The announcement in the July 1913 Fenton Independent read:

## McWilliams–Scott Wedding

*A wedding of interest to Fenton people took place Saturday, when Mrs. Grace Colwell Scott was married to Rev. John R. McWilliams, pastor of the Presbyterian Church. The wedding took place at the parsonage which has been lately refurnished. The ceremony was performed by a friend of the groom, Rev. E. H. Bradfield of Lapeer. Miss Lizzie Jennings played the Wedding March. The appointments were pink and white, and pink roses gave a brilliant touch to the decorations. The bride was gowned in white crepe de chine, trimmed with lace. She was unattended. A luncheon was served in the dining room, where the color scheme was artistically carried out. The guests were Mrs. Hattie Colwell and sons, John and Bruce, of Ithaca; Mr. and Mrs. Heber Curtis and daughter, Mildred, of Linden; Mr. and Mrs. John Colwell, parents of the bride; Mr. and Mrs. Charlie Scott. The bride is the daughter of Mr. and Mrs. John Colwell of this place and is well known in Fenton social circles. The groom for this last year has been the pastor of Fenton Presbyterian Church. Mr. and Mrs. McWilliams left for a short wedding trip.*

It was a small wedding. So small that Billie age 7 and Helen age 10 did not attend. Afterwards they stayed with Grandma and Grandpa Colwell for a few weeks. When they returned, it was to a new house. The manse was halfway between their old Victorian on Shiawassee Avenue and Grandpa's brick home on High Street. Helen and Billie had a new house, new neighbors, new friends, and also a new school, South Ward. Billie's little sweetheart, Nellie, still attended North Ward, and opportunities to see her were fewer. On Sunday mornings, from the family pew in the Presbyterian Church, Billie watched Nellie play outside after services at St. Jude's Episcopal. He never wavered in his affection. Nellie would always be his girl.

There were three ward schools in the village, all identical two-story brick buildings. Inside the entryway of South Ward School were hooks where hats and jackets were hung. The school was heated by a coal stove on each floor. In the front hall was a cast iron sink with a tin drinking cup, and out back were two outhouses, one for the girls and one for the boys. Inside the main room, a large blackboard stood behind the teacher's desk. The school day opened with a song and a prayer. Recess was held at 10:30 and an hour break was given at noon. Most children walked home for lunch.

Children began their education in "chart class," where the youngest learned the alphabet and simple sight words. From there, they advanced to first grade. Chart class, first and second grade were on the first floor. Third and fourth grade were upstairs. Fenton's fifth and sixth graders were in a combined class at West Ward School. Billie was glad of that, because it meant that he and Nellie would be in class together again.

Billie, now seven years old, adjusted quickly to the new school, but it took some time for him to become friends with his new stepfather. At first, Reverend Mac bided his time and let Grace continue as the disciplinarian. One night at dinner, however, he reached a breaking point, and the family dynamic changed.

"Billie, please sit still at the table!" Grace said to her restless son.

He continued to fidget.

"Billie!" she admonished him again, exasperated.

Grace was used to scolding Billie repeatedly, but the Reverend had reached his limit. One of Grace's old riding whips hung on the dining room wall. Reverend Mac sprung up from the table, took hold of Billie with one hand and grabbed the old riding whip with the other. The loud crack of the whip as it met Billie's behind startled them all. Reverend Mac was awful strong when he got mad.

After a moment, Billie noticed that he wasn't in much pain. He looked at his stepfather examining the broken whip with a puzzled expression. The leather on the old whip was rotted and it had broken as soon as it touched Billie's behind.

"Let that be a lesson to you, young man," said the Reverend sternly looking down at the boy and laying the whip on the table top.

"Yes, sir," replied Billie.

"I'd not like to break another whip on your backside," continued the Reverend.

Billie heard the softening of the Reverend's voice and saw a smile in the man's eyes. They had reached an unspoken understanding that night and were to become great friends. Soon after, Billie and Helen started calling their stepfather Dad Mac.

One day the following summer, Dad Mac spent the morning working on the car, getting it ready to take the family to the circus. Billie watched the process with interest. When the work was done, Billie proudly presented Dad Mac with a cigar.

"Uncle Charlie told me to give it to you," he said.

Dad Mac smiled and lit the cigar. It exploded! After the shock, he glared at Billie, his head covered with tobacco and ashes. "If you want to go to the circus, go ask your uncle Charlie to take you!" he snarled.

Billie was speechless. His lip began to tremble. "I didn't ...I didn't...," he stammered.

Suddenly, Dad Mac realized Billie had been duped too. He rubbed the soot off his face with his handkerchief and picked the boy up. "All right, we'll go to the circus today," he said. "But mind you—we'll take care of your uncle next week!"

Grace felt fortunate to share her life with Mac. He was a loving husband, a real gentleman and a fine preacher. Each Sunday, he gave a simple message based on the scripture for the day. Never writing his sermons word for word, he preached from an outline marked with colored pencils. His congregation, especially the children, loved him, and Billie enjoyed an enhanced status among his friends with Mac as his dad. As he got older, Billie especially liked riding with his stepdad on house calls. It was great to have Mac's undivided attention for long talks in the car.

Days at the manse always began with Bible readings and prayers, but Dad Mac saw to it that Helen and Billie never missed the circus and other fun activities. This wasn't easy on his salary of $600 per year. Grace, the perfect minister's wife, managed to deftly manipulate the family budget so it always balanced.

Years of being on her own had taught her household budgeting.

Mac routinely received calls to other churches, but always turned them down. He rejected one because "they had too heavy an endowment" and a large campus. He explained to his wife that he was more comfortable in a modest church. When he was called by a small, growing congregation in the town of Redford, however, he accepted. World War I had just ended and northwest Detroit was booming. This church and the town were more to his liking.

The days of wagons and teams were fading fast, and the move to Redford was by truck. Twelve-year-old Billie was excited to go with Dad Mac and the truck driver. He sat on the floor with his feet hanging out the back of the truck. What an adventure.

Grace and Helen took the train to Pontiac, then boarded the electric interurban car to Redford. New wooden floors were being installed so all the furniture from the manse was in the garage. The only items in the house were a few sawhorses with planks laid on top. Grace hadn't expected this. Not to be deterred, she covered the planks with paper and set the "table" with linen napkins and a bouquet of flowers, ready to serve her family's first dinner in their new home. When he saw the spread of chicken sandwiches and sliced fruit, Dad Mac smiled in appreciation of his wife's ingenuity. But where were they going to sleep?

At the end of the meal, they heard a noise outside. Billie hopped up and peered out the window.

"Wow! You should see this automobile!" he shouted.

It was Mr. Bosworth, a man from the congregation, in a sleek Nash touring car. After being invited inside, he apologized for the delay in meeting them.

"I meant to intercept you before you saw the condition of the house," he explained. "Mrs. Bosworth and I want to invite you to live with us until the work on the manse is complete."

"That's very kind of you," Grace said with barely concealed relief. Eating at sawhorses was one thing, but creating beds in an empty house would have been a bit more difficult.

Mr. and Mrs. Bosworth had a beautiful home, and their hospitality gave the McWilliams no reason to hurry the workmen. Finally, however, it was moving day. Early in the morning, the family went to get their furniture out of the garage and begin the work of moving in. To their shock, the garage was empty.

"Oh, John," cried Grace. "What are we going-" she stopped when she saw Mr. Bosworth laughing. It wasn't a robbery—the neighbors had done the work the night before, even setting up the beds. Billie heard cackling.

"Chickens!" cried Billie and Helen at the same time and raced into the backyard. There was a chicken coop in the back as well, already housing chickens. Happy and grateful, the family felt very welcome in their new home.

Billie had left behind a lucrative job as a paperboy for the Flint Journal, but he knew he could find something similar in Redford. Hopefully, he would net $3 to $4 per week, as he had done in Fenton. The Detroit Free Press was sold on the street corner in Redford where the Detroit Interurban stopped. The newsboys would grab an armful of papers at 4 AM and board the car going into the city. They would sell papers to the commuters until the next stop. The tips were good— usually five cents for the three-cent paper. It was a tough way to make money, however. By the time Billie started school every morning, he was exhausted. Dad Mac could see the toll this schedule was having on the twelve-year-old. While work was important, school was even more so. If Billie wanted to work, he needed to find a new job—one that wouldn't tire him out so much that he couldn't study.

A solution came when Mac introduced Billie to a lady from the congregation who lived alone. Billie became her all-around handyman: scrubbing floors, washing windows, firing furnaces, mowing the lawn, and cleaning the walk. The hours were flexible and the pay was good. This became his favorite job, in part because the lady was a cousin to Mrs. Clara Ford,

FIRST PRESBYTERIAN CHURCH, FENTON, MICH.

First Presbyterian Church. Photo courtesy of A J Phillips Historical Museum

Henry Ford's wife. Billie loved to listen to her stories about Henry Ford and his inventions. He was fascinated by Ford's first car, the Quadricycle which was basically two bicycles with a seat. She also told him how he was speeding up the manufacture of his Model T car using a moving assembly line. She often told him Ford would say, "If you think you can do a thing or think you can't do a thing, you're right" and "Failure is simply the opportunity to begin again, this time more intelligently." Billie took these words to heart.

# 30
## The Senior Dance

1922

**Senior Dance Fenton High School**

Grace told her son about the letter as soon as he walked in the house that afternoon. Bill figured it could only be from one person, as he didn't get many letters. He picked up the creamy white envelope from the top of his bureau and stared at Nellie's neat cursive handwriting with trepidation. Without opening it, Bill carefully laid the letter back on the bureau and sat on the edge of the bed to think. Was she breaking it off with him? His friend George had written as much a few months ago.

"You don't need to keep writing to Nellie," George's letter said, the smug words practically oozing off the page. "She's my girl now."

No, Bill wouldn't believe that until he heard it from Nellie herself. None of the girls at Redford High School could hold a candle to her. She was the only girl for him. It seemed like he had known that fact all his life, starting with the North Ward School days when he pushed her on the swing before class, to the afternoons of leafing through the Montgomery Ward catalogue picking out furniture for their future home.

But then his family moved to Redford. He'd been back every summer to visit, but knew he wasn't Nellie's only suitor. There were more rivals than just George. After all, wouldn't every guy be after the most wonderful girl in the world?

Bill stood and picked the envelope up again. He was reluctant to read what Nellie had to say, but he had to find out. Carefully, he slit the envelope open and pulled out the thin, delicate paper. Only one page!

He read through the letter carefully, read it again, then sunk back down on the bed with a sigh of relief. Nellie wasn't breaking up with him. She had invited to him to the Senior Dance at Fenton High School!

Excited, Bill rushed to tell his mother, who was glad for the news. She knew he had always been sweet on Nellie Phillips. Bill and Dad Mac checked the train schedules to find the best route. The CN Line, which ran up through Pontiac and Holly to Fenton, was most direct. If Bill caught the 2:30, he'd arrive in plenty of time. A two-hour layover in Pontiac was scheduled, but that route still beat the other trains.

Bill wrote ahead to let Nellie know when he was coming. He also wrote to Grandma and Grandpa Colwell to be sure he could stay with them. He could hardly wait for the weekend to arrive.

Early Saturday afternoon, he caught the trolley and rode it down to the Detroit Michigan Central Train Depot. There had been many newspaper stories when the huge depot was finished in 1913, but reading about it had not prepared Bill for the grandeur in front of him now. Designed in the Beaux Art style, the train station was the most imposing and beautiful building he had ever seen.

In front of the building, Roosevelt Park was almost completed. The huge grassy expanse was lined with trees and streetlights and flanked by wide roadways on either side. Beyond the park, Michigan Central rose up a towering 230 feet, comprised of both the train station and a thirteen-story office building. A massive marquee decorated the depot's main entrance, made up of three huge doors. Above each door were three large and two smaller arched windows. Bill felt dwarfed as he walked up to the entrance and pushed the heavy door open.

Inside, Doric columns, almost fifty-five feet tall, rose from the polished marble floors to the arched ceilings. The ticket counters were across the lobby. Above them, a huge clock was mounted on the Kasota marble wall. Bill purchased his round-trip ticket and walked to the crowded waiting room, filled with row after row of Indian mahogany benches. He had thirty minutes before his train left so Bill decided to explore this incredible building while he waited.

First, he walked past the concession stand in the main waiting room and down the brick-walled concourse filled with arcade shops. Light poured in from the huge copper skylight in the ceiling. There was a newsstand, a drugstore, a cigar shop and a barber shop. There was also a separate women's waiting room with leather rocking chairs, shiny wood floors, enormous potted plants and light-filled arched windows. He then passed an L-shaped lunch counter with more than twenty round soda stools, then a formal dining room with a vaulted Caen stone ceiling and a Welsh quarry tile floor. The tables were set with white linen tablecloths and each had a crystal water decanter.

Bill checked his watch and made his way down the ramp to the train platforms. The noise was incredible, as was the crush of people. Along the ten pairs of tracks were ten passenger platforms on each side and another five island platforms. Immediately outside there were seven additional freight tracks and one mail track. Signage was lacking, but a train conductor stood at the foot of the wrought iron stairs directing passengers. He showed Bill where to board his train.

The trip was without incident until Bill got to Pontiac and the two-hour layover. *I've got plenty of time to kill* he thought so he decided to pay a quick visit to an old friend from Redford High School who had moved to Pontiac the year before. Bill chatted pleasantly with the girl and her family until he looked at his watch. He only had ten minutes to catch his train! Panic set in.

"I've got to run!" he cried and raced out the door. He was only a couple blocks from the train station, but he felt like he was in a bad dream, everything moving in slow motion. He dodged in and out of pedestrians on the sidewalk and bolted through traffic at an intersection. Out of breath he ran towards the passenger platform just as his train pulled away.

"Stop! Stop!" he yelled, waving his arms, but to no avail. He slowed down and watched the caboose moving away from him. Dashing into the depot he checked the schedule. The next train would not be leaving for over an hour. He sat down hard on a wooden chair in the waiting room. He was not leaving this spot even for a minute until the next train arrived.

It was very late when Bill finally arrived in Fenton. Nellie's father was waiting with his car.

"My goodness, Bill, what happened? We've been worried. You're so late."

Bill was chagrined. His stomach was one giant knot. "I'm so sorry, Mr. Phillips. I-I missed my connection in Pontiac. I didn't mean to make everyone worry," he sputtered.

"Well how did that happen?" Clifford Phillips reproached him. "I thought you had plenty of time in Pontiac. I told Nellie not to wait, so she's already gone to the dance. I'll take you there directly."

Just when he thought things could not get any worse, Bill realized not only was he late, but he wasn't dressed for the dance.

"Mr. Phillips, would you mind if we stopped by my grandparents so I can change my clothes real quick? I don't want to embarrass Nellie any more than I already have."

On the short drive, Bill explained what had happened. "I'm so sorry I made everyone worry. I just lost track of time," he explained. Mr. Phillips just nodded. Once he had changed clothes they headed over to the school. When Bill walked into the gymnasium he paused and scanned the crowd looking for Nellie. Where was she? He spotted his old friend George first, laughing and talking to a girl. It was Nellie. Just then she looked up and noticing him, beamed.

"Bill!" she cried and scampered over, leaving George behind. "You made it after all. I was so worried." She grabbed his hands and leaned in and pecked him on the cheek.

The evening turned out to be a smash. Bill was thrilled to be there with his girl. Yes, his girl! His old friends from grammar school—including George—looked on with envy as Bill danced the night away with his Nellie. They had a wonderful time.

The next morning, Bill felt like he was on top of the world. He'd been invited to breakfast at the Phillips' before he caught the train back to Detroit. Whistling, he bounded up the stone steps two at a time and rapped on the front door. Mr. Phillips opened the door and held it for Bill to come in.

"Hello, Bill. Nice to see you again. Come on in." Mr. Phillips was as reserved and polite as ever.

Bill stepped in and looked around expectantly for Nellie. He wanted to spend as much time as possible with her before he left for home.

"Nellie is still upstairs, Bill. I'm sure she'll be down shortly."

The table in the dining room was already laid out for breakfast. Bill could smell the eggs and rashers cooking. Mrs. Phillips came out of the kitchen, wiping her hands on her apron. She glanced at her husband and then back at Bill.

"Good morning, Bill. Would you like to sit down and have some coffee?"

The coffee was poured. Minutes ticked by. No Nellie. The Phillips politely inquired about Bill's folks and his sister. Bill answered, but sat on the edge of his seat, his leg jiggling nervously. Finally, Mrs. Phillips called upstairs.

"Nellie! Can you come down, Dear? Bill is here and we're waiting for you for breakfast."

Bill could hear a door open and footsteps on the stairs. He stood up. Nellie stopped at the bottom of the staircase and glared at him. "Well. Good morning, Bill. Nice to see you again."

So polite and cold! Bill was confused. What could have happened just overnight? Everything had gone so well at the dance. Now it was obvious that Nellie had a change of heart!

They all sat at the big table in the dining room. Nellie carefully set her napkin on her lap. She picked up her table knife and daintily tapped it against the shell of the soft boiled egg in the egg cup in front of her. The top of the shell came off easily. Bill just watched her. Finally, she looked up at Bill and said sweetly, "So how is your friend in Pontiac?"

After the awkward breakfast and Nellie's icy goodbye to Bill, Clifford regretted having told his daughter the reason Bill had been late to the dance. He hadn't expected her to be so upset. Didn't she know she was the only girl for Bill? Everyone else could see it. Bill always had a crush on Nellie, he chuckled to himself, right from the day she was born.

But being late for the dance because he stopped to see another girl had hurt Nellie's feelings. Clifford had underestimated how angry his daughter would be. He liked Bill and Bill's family and hoped he might be able to fix this.

He waited a few hours before retrieving a small blue box from his bureau and going up to Nellie's bedroom. He rapped on the door and a very quiet voice said "Come in." Nellie sat on her bed, her face tear stained. Clifford sat beside her on the bed.

"Maybe I shouldn't have told you," he said. "I'm sorry."

Nellie shook her head. "No. I'm glad you did. It's better I know before I make a lifelong mistake."

Clifford sighed. "Well, I don't think it's as serious as all that. I really do think Bill was quite innocent in stopping off to see a friend. He wouldn't have told me if he had something to hide, would he?"

"Really?" Nellie exclaimed. "He thought it was perfectly fine to stop and see another girl and be late for a date with me! And not just any date, but the Senior Dance? I guess I should have just gone with George and let Bill have fun in Redford with his new friends."

Clifford held out the small blue box and opened it. Inside was the gold and silver lover's knot ring his mother had given him years ago before he left for England. How it brought back memories!

"I do hope that's not a peace offering from Bill," Nellie said flatly.

"No, not at all. This ring has been in our family for a long time. My mother gave it to me before your mother and I were married. She said it was a lover's knot, and the gold and silver are two separate threads that intertwine to form the perfect knot. She told me to think about that when I chose the woman I wanted to spend the rest of my life with—to be sure that person complemented me. I was convinced your mother was the one for me, but the ring was a good reminder."

He handed his daughter the ring. "Nellie, I hope you are as lucky in love as your mother and I have been. Think about it carefully. You don't want to have any regrets."

# 31
## *A Hard Worker*

1914—1925

Bill could never remember being without a job. He started while he was still in knickers, picking up scrap iron from his neighbors with his red coaster wagon and selling it for 10 cents a load to the local foundry foreman.

At home, he learned to take over the chores that a man would do, chopping wood for the kitchen stove and fireplace and maintaining the furnace and hot water stove. He worked for the neighbors washing windows, weeding gardens, raking leaves, cleaning snow off walks and carrying out ashes. By the time he could wear long pants, he was paying for his own clothes and expenses.

Nellie Phillips

In 1914, at the age of eight, Bill was offered a job as a newsboy for the Flint Journal. He quickly expanded his routes and became a territory leader. After his mother married Reverend McWilliams, Bill took over the janitorial work at the church, building the fire in the furnace before Sunday services.

Bill was always on the lookout for an opportunity. In high school, he heard Grand Lawn Cemetery was being enlarged and was hired as a water boy. On Christmas vacations, he pumped out portable toilets. During one spring vacation, he was hired to help re-do the tennis courts.

After high school, Bill began seminary studies at Alma College. He admired his stepdad, Rev. Mac, so much that he wanted to follow in his footsteps. Nellie was in nursing school at the University of Michigan in Ann Arbor. He needed to work for tuition and bills, he missed Nellie and traveled to see her on weekends, and his grades suffered. Bill had indeed spread himself too thin. He ended his first semester on probation! He had never failed at anything before. Something had to give. He decided to transfer to the University of Michigan to study mechanical engineering.

Bill Scott

# 32
# A Thanksgiving Wedding

NOVEMBER 24, 1927

It was Thanksgiving Day —and also Bill's wedding day—but he could not have felt more forlorn. He and his best man, Jack Book, stood by the ditch next to their Tin Lizzie. Bill had wanted this day to be perfect. He had certainly waited long enough. But it was not to be. As Jack was driving, he tried to negotiate a curve a little too quickly and they had slid into the ditch. It was not exactly Jack's fault, Bill told himself. They were late and Bill was urging him to go faster.

Initially, the two young men tried to push the car out by themselves, without getting their clothing too soiled. Eventually they agreed they would have to resort to calling Bill's stepfather, Dad Mac. Nellie's father, Clifford Phillips, was also coming to help extract the car from the ditch and bring them back to the house for the wedding. It was not the first time Bill had been embarrassed in front of Nellie's father. Things couldn't be worse, thought Bill with a sigh. The only consolation was that this time it wasn't another girl who made him late.

Although Bill was sure that Nellie was the girl for him, he sometimes wondered if Nellie's father had doubts. After all, it had been a long-distance relationship since Bill's family had moved from Fenton to Redford while they were still in elementary school. Bill winced, thinking of the Senior Dance fiasco. Nellie never failed to bring it up when they argued. He was certain her father still remembered too.

Dad Mac and Mr. Phillips were grim when they arrived. They had been waiting at the Phillips' house for Bill and Jack so the ceremony could begin. Needless to say, Nellie and her mother were upset. The guests were whispering. No one quite knew what to make of Bill's absence. The atmosphere was tense when Bill finally called. Surveying the accident they decided to leave the Model T in the ditch and head back to the house in Dad Mac's car. It was a quiet trip.

Nellie waited patiently up in her bedroom. Mabel had come in to explain the delay to her daughter but then she went downstairs to mingle with the guests. It would not do for the guests to see Nellie before the wedding ceremony. She looked around her bedroom, acutely aware that she was leaving her childhood home for good. She smoothed the pink flowered comforter and reminisced. She looked around at her childhood possessions: her little wooden doll bed, her bisque dolls, her blue and white tea set, the small steamer trunk where she stored her doll clothes, and the Lane hope chest. Her eyes rested on the ring box sitting on her dressing table. She paused, remembering another time Bill had kept her waiting. She walked over and opened the box to look at the silver and gold ring resting on the white satin. She remembered how heart-broken she felt after the Senior Dance. She had always considered Bill to be her beau, and her's alone. It had been a shock that he had even paid attention to another girl. She could have played it safe with George. He'd made it clear he was interested. But she always knew that Bill was the only one for her. How often she'd heard

Nellie Phillips

the story that they had met the day she was born. Of course, he was only a couple weeks old at the time. She smiled at the memory, shook her head and closed the ring box. Now, he was keeping her waiting again. Nellie was happier than she had ever been, but she felt anxious, too. Bill still had the last year of college to complete. She would be proud to wear her wedding ring but in a few days it would have to go on the chain around her neck, out of view, if she wanted to keep her job. Nurses were not allowed to be married. Life with Bill would never be dull, that's for sure.

Bill stood in the Phillips' front room in front of the minister, his best man Jack by his side. He smoothed his hair and rocked nervously on his feet. Miss Alice Van Atta sat at the piano and after a nod from Mabel began playing the wedding march. Clifford started down the stairs, his only daughter on his arm. Nellie was dressed in a stylish pink flapper dress with a cloche hat on her short dark hair. Bill remembered he had compliment-ed Nellie on her hair when it was long. So many girls were wearing the new short bobs. Then he made the mistake of admonishing her to never cut it. She promptly did, and he knew he had met his match. Looking at his beautiful bride, Bill knew he could ask for nothing more. He would do anything for her.

# Bessie's Letter

Grandpa Phillips (given name Charles), was a farmer living in the vicinity of Highland and Milford. I have no idea where he was born, or the names of his parents, but they probably came from New England.

He was married four times, and all four wives are buried with him in the cemetery near Highland. I do not know his first wife's name, but four children were born to them: Charles, Andrew Jackson, and Alva, and one daughter, Emily. There may have been more, but those are the ones I remember. Charlie went out to western Canada, and I believe he married a girl named Morse, for they had a son named Morse Phillips. Uncle Andrew and Uncle Alvie lived on the Avenue (Shiawassee), and Aunt Emily's home was on Adelaide St., the first house south of Elizabeth St., on the east side of the street. Your grandpa, Judson, built the house for her, just the way she wanted it, and she was so proud of it. She was one of the dearest people I knew in my childhood. She was strict Baptist, as were all the Phillips family, and I can see her yet, dressed for church, with her pretty black bonnet, tied under her chin.

I do not know if Judson's mother was Grandpa's second or third wife, but I do know her maiden name was Electa Mudge, and her home was near Caro Michigan. She had a brother, Charles, who frequently came to visit us. The last time when he was quite old, and I was about eleven years old. It didn't make the least difference to any of the family in their affection and relationship to our mother when she married again after Judson passed on. They all came to our house frequently, and we often visited them. In fact, the only playmates I had when I was a child, besides my own cousins, were Harry Phillips' girls, Marjorie and Lucy, and occasionally Robert, Ashley's youngest son. Marjorie and Lucy and I were constant companions.

Before I forget, I must tell you that the Mudge family were part Indian. Of what tribe, or how much, no one ever said, but it was an acknowledged fact. Grandpa Phillips loved Electa very much, and he gave specific orders that he was to be buried beside her when he died.

Grandpa's last wife was Betsey Lovejoy, and she outlived him by a number of years.

I think Aunt Emily was the one who brought Judson up. She adored him, and he felt the same way about her. When he was in his early twenties he went out west, to Washington, and worked for a big lumber company for some time. Later he came to Fenton and joined his half-brothers in the factory. He became superintendent, and patented several ideas on the manufacture of the window screens, etc. In reality, it was he who made the Phillips factory the success it grew to be.

A short while before he died he made Uncle Andrew's oldest son, Win, executor of his estate. Our mother begged him to appoint someone else, the only time she ever disputed his judgment, but he laughed at her, and told her Winnie was a good, honest man, and would look out for her interests. As it turned out, she was right, because Win short-changed her in many ways, the cruelest of which was when the patents ran out, instead of renewing them in her name, he put them in his name. And he never offered compensation for the thousands of dollars they were worth. Her own lawyer was ill at the time, so she went to Everett Scott (Bill's father), a young lawyer who had just come to Fenton and opened his office. He advised her not to do anything about it, as it would stir up so much unpleasantness. She always felt that he thought it wise not to get himself "in wrong" with such an influential family if he was going to be a successful attorney. She always regretted that she didn't consult someone in Flint or Detroit. It would have meant comfort instead of the hardship she knew in later life. She always thought a great deal of the other two boys, Ashley and Harry, especially Ashley.

Shortly after coming to Fenton he met our mother while attending a social function of some kind. From then on, he tried in every way to get her attention, but she avoided him. She was only seventeen, and she had a sweetheart she was very much in love with, who had moved to Oakland, California with his parents a short time before. They had been sweet-hearts since the fifth grade, all through high school, up until the senior year when he left. Finally, when Judson (she always called him "Juddy") did break down her resistance, she told him he would be wasting his time, and why. He told her that was just "puppy love" and she would laugh about it in later years. As it happened, the California boyfriend had one of these socially minded mothers and she had her eyes on a perfect match for her son, an only daughter of a very wealthy San Francisco financier. So she deftly intercepted the sweetheart's correspondence, and made it known, through mutual friends that her son had found someone else. At first our mother was heartbroken, but shortly her pride came to the rescue and she started accepting Juddy's attentions. Besides it was rather gratifying to take the handsome young man all the other girls were trying their best to ensnare out of circulation. And she never regretted marrying him for a single minute. He was a wonderful husband, and she was always so proud of him. The only fault she ever found with him was that he never taught her anything about business.

He did all the buying, even to outfitting family with clothing in the spring and fall. They would go to Detroit and he would buy much more expensive things than she would dream of, and more of them. At home, he had a purse up in the cupboard where he put the money for the household expenses—so much for the milk, so much for this, and so much for that. So when he was gone, she had no idea of how to manage, and she made a dreadful mess of the money she could have enjoyed in comfort all her life.

When they were first married they rented the house in the middle of the block, on the west side of Adelaide, between Elizabeth St. and Rockwell. Nellie was born there in that house. Later they bought the big, square house on west Caroline St., the first house west of Adelaide, on the south side of the street. Your father was born there. Then a few years later they bought the house on the corner of Shiawassee and Adelaide, (our "House on the Corner" that we all loved dearly), where Juddy died May 30, 1894, of tuberculosis, after several years of ill health. It was Memorial Day, with a big parade, and the band playing, and of course they always marched up the Avenue to the cemetery, but it seemed to her, even years afterward, that it was a sacrilege to celebrate that day, even in memoriam.

In March, 1896, she married my father, Hadley Gould, son of Reuben and Ruth (McWain) Gould of South Grand Blanc and brother of Dr. Jefferson Gould of Fenton. The next December, 29th, I was born and seven years later on July 25th, Kenneth was born.

Nellie graduated as valedictorian of her class a few days before her 17th birthday, which was June 30th. She attended the University of Michigan for several months, until her health began to fail. A physical exam revealed symptoms of tuberculosis, and she came home. Uncle Jeff (Dr. Gould) advised her to take plenty of rest, and eat plenty of good nourishing food, and by fall she was much better. Mamma had an artist friend, Nina Booth, of whom she had taken oil and pastel painting lessons, who lived in Florida, and with the doctor's advice she enrolled at the Stetson University in Delan, Florida. She played the organ at the Baptist church there, and that was where she met Nellie Teale's father, Fred Donovan. He was young minister, just beginning to preach. They were married in November of 1899, and Nellie (Teale) was born the 13th of the following September, in Colorado Springs, Colorado. Our Nellie lived just four days after her baby was born, and died Sept. 17, 1900. They had gone to Colorado hoping her health would improve, and it probably would have if she hadn't been pregnant. All this while she and Fred had been living on her monthly allowance from her share of her father's estate. Aunt Julia Phillips had been appointed guardian of both Nellie's and Clifford's estate, and they had a very generous allowance that paid all their expenses wherever they were.

Fred brought the baby straight home to Mamma, but when he found that he wasn't to get Nellie's inheritance, he promptly took the baby away, and Mamma wasn't allowed to see her (if Fred knew it), until she went to live with the Furnesses in Indianapolis. Juddy (Nellie's father) had made no provision in his will for grandchildren. According to the will, Mamma, Nellie and Clifford were to each get one third of the estate, but their shares (Nellie's and Clifford's) were to be held in trust until Clifford was twenty-one. As Nellie was only twenty when she died, a separate guardian had to be appointed for her baby. Her allowance went right on, for the baby's care, until it was twenty-one, and then it would inherit the estate. Lou LaTourette was appointed her guardian, but Clifford was the executor, so when she, Nellie Teale, was twenty-one he turned it all over to her.

When Clifford was fourteen or fifteen years old, Aunt Julia persuaded Mamma to send him to the military academy at Orchard Lake. (That is where he developed that beautiful straight back and soldierly walk. Burns Fuller called it "the Phillip's walk". Well it wasn't. Uncle Andrew and Win just stuck out their bay-windows and strutted. There was a world of difference, believe me.)

I don't know how long he went to Orchard Lake, but when Nellie was in Florida he attended a boy's school there; and for a while he went to a school in Kalamazoo. That could have been while she was attending the U of M. When she was in Colorado he went to a school near Colorado Springs named Hagerman Hall. Then, after all that, he came back home and graduated from Fenton High, when he was twenty-one or -two. For a graduation gift, Aunt Julia sent him on the trip to England along with Allen Gunning, who was going back for a visit with his mother and other members of the family. That was in 1904, and Kenneth was born while he was in England.

Win built the big house just east of your house, and he and his wife Sarah had just one child, a daughter, Julia, who married a man named Charles Hart. They had four daughters, and the last I knew, Julia lived in, or near Ann Arbor. Mr. Hart committed suicide when the girls were small.

Harry and his wife Georgia lived in an older house where the Neeley's now live. Harry built that lovely home about 1905 or 1906. They had lived there only about a year when their oldest little girl, Marjorie, died of diphtheria. It was the year when antitoxin was first used as a remedy for diphtheria, and although Harry and Georgie had specialists from Detroit, and trained nurses for

Marjorie, she was given an overdose of anti-toxin, and died. She was eight years old April 15 and she died shortly after school started in the fall. I remember we were in the third grade.

Ashley's home was the house on the south-west corner of Adelaide and Rockwell streets until he built the stone house on Shiawassee Ave., where I believe someone named Bigelow lives now. He was the father of Donald and Robert, and his wife's name was Louise, but we always just called her "Lou".

I didn't know Win and Sarah very well, as they were much older, but I knew Ashley and Lou since I was a baby, and Harry and Georgie even better. And all of us (meaning Ashley and Lou's children) played at Aunt Julia's as she was their grandma, and they all called her "Mam'er", and I called her "Aunt Julia" the same as Clifford and Nellie did. I thought she was my aunt, too, and she never told me that she wasn't. She always gave me Christmas and birthday presents, signed "From Aunt Julia", and even when my Bob was born, she and Aunt Lottie walked over to call and see the baby, and brought him presents, from "Aunt Julia, and Aunt Charlotte". They were always a part of my family, and very good to me.

The next time I see you, Juddy, I will fill in all the details, but as you know, "times a-wastin'" and at least you know this much about your father's people.

With love,

Bessie

# *Appendix*

### Daniel Colwell (1876 – 1944)

Daniel Colwell was born to David Colwell and Phoebe Colwell when they were ages fifty–one & forty–six, respectively. He married Anna Golden from Petoskey on November 15, 1899 and they had five children: Grace, Margaret, David, Ruth and Meris. In 1910, he left for Alaska and never returned. Anna divorced him, probably for desertion, and moved back to Petoskey. While in Alaska, Daniel claimed to be single and shaved years off his age. He worked as a hunter and trapper in Ft. Gibbon and in 1930 married Agnes, who was a native Eskimo/Indian. They had one daughter, Phoebe. According to the census he was a grocer.

### Ray Edison Corrigan (1891 – 1945)

Ray served in WWI as a pilot in the U.S. Army Air Service and was awarded the WWI Victory Medal and Victory Button. Both were bronze which meant he was not injured. He enlisted on November 7, 1917 and took ground training at Camp Dix in Ithaca, New York. He was appointed Second Lieutenant July 29, 1918 and send to Rockwell Field August 8, 1918 for his primary training. He finished his training at Call Field in Texas and October 1918 he was sent to Langley Field in Hampton, Virginia and then Taliaferro Field in Hicks, Texas. He received a "Certificate of Graduation" from the Air Service Flying School, Langley Field, Hampton, Virginia November 19, 1918. January 10, 1919, he was honorably discharged from the Air Service Aeronautics of the United States Army, Flying Cadet Signal–Enlisted Reserve Corps in Taliaferro Field, Hicks, Ft. Worth, Texas. Unfortunately, his military records at the National Archives were destroyed in a fire in 1973. He and Clara Forte married in St. John's Episcopal Church in Ithaca, New York while he was an aviation cadet. After the war, he met the Dodge brothers in Michigan and they convinced him to open a Dodge Dealership in Glendale, California. Ray and Clara had two daughters,

Margaret and Elizabeth. After the war, he continued to fly demonstrations and acrobatics at county fairs. He belonged to Oakmont Country Club in Glendale, California.

### Nellie Donovan Teale (1900 – 1992)

Nellie was the daughter of Nellie Phillips and Fred Donovan. Her mother died three days after she was born and she was raised by the Furness family in Indianapolis, Indiana. She married Edwin Way Teale and traveled with him extensively with his work as a naturalist, author and photographer, documenting environmental conditions across North America 1930–1980. He won a Pulitzer Prize in 1966 for his book "Wandering through Winter." She remained friends with her cousin Nellie Geraldine Phillips Scott and her husband William C. Scott.

### Marjorie Marshall Phillips (1898 – 1905)

Daughter of Harry Judson Phillips and Georgia Marshall Phillips, Marjorie contacted diphtheria when she was eight years old. It was the first year an antitoxin was used as a remedy for diphtheria. Her parents brought in specialists and trained nurses from Detroit for Marjorie. Even so, she was given an overdose of the antitoxin and died.

### Horace Rackham (1858 – 1933) & Mary Horton Rackham (1864 – 1946)

Horace Rackham is a name well-known throughout Michigan. There are Rackham buildings on the campuses of the University of Michigan, Eastern Michigan University and Wayne State University. Rackham donated the land for the Detroit Zoo, and the Rackham Golf Course and clubhouse to the city of Detroit.

Horace Rackham moved to Detroit in 1879 after graduating from high school in Leslie, Michigan. He worked for the Berry Brothers Varnish Inc. while studying law under Adolph Sloman and Edward Kane. In 1884, he was admitted to the bar and the next year married Mary Horton from Fenton,

Michigan. He was not in good health but he loved the outdoors. He and Mary purchased an eight–acre truck farm south of Fenton where he recuperated from his poor health. In 1887, he and Mary had the Fenton Fire Hall built as a gift to the village. In 1894, he was practicing law with John H. Anderson. His fortune really began in 1903. Anderson brought in a client, Alexander Malcomson, who was a prosperous coal merchant. Malcomson knew Henry Ford well and was a backer of his new company. He brought Ford to Rackham's law firm. At the time Horace Rackham and Henry Ford were not acquainted but their wives were friends and neighbors on W. Alexandrine Avenue. They visited almost daily. Horace was hired to draw up the papers of incorporation for Ford Motor Co. Against the advice of his banker, he invested $5,000 in fifty shares of the company and was elected Chairman. In 1907, Horace built his home at 90 Edison which still stands. Ford built a house at 140 Edison a year later. In 1919, Edsel Ford bought back the stock back from Rackham for $12.5 million. The Rackhams had no children. They were a handsome but quiet couple. He was tall and distinguished–looking and she was petite and soft–featured. They had a small circle of close friends and were avid golfers. Mary had graduated from finishing school and was a tremendous influence on Horace. She was an accomplished pianist and belonged to the Shakespeare Study club. The couple were members of the Detroit Symphony Society. Although born a Presbyterian, Mary became interested in Christian Science and they both joined the Christian Science Church. Because of their religious convictions and Horace's retiring nature and need for privacy, many of the Rackham donations were made anonymously.

In 1934 the Rackham Trust was established. Among the donations to Fenton were the Community Center, a pipe organ to the Presbyterian Church and a church building and pipe organ to the Christian Science Church.

The trustees included Bryson D. Horton (Mary's brother), Myrna Horton Bussey (Mary's sister), and Frederick G. Rolland (married to Mary's best friend Margaret Eddy.) Each of these trustees was already quite successful in their own right.

Upon Mary Rackham's death, the home at 90 Edison was deeded to Nellie G. Phillips Scott in exchange for "love." She owned it until 1977. This is where my mother, Shirley Scott, lived with her family while she attended Wayne State University. Upon her marriage to my father, Jim McKeon, they lived in the two–bedroom apartment over the carriage house. My brother and I were both born there.

### William C & Nellie G Scott

Bill and Nellie were married for over 60 years. To the day he died, Bill claimed he knew Nellie was the girl for him since they met on the day she was born. And Nellie never let him forget why he had been late to the Senior Dance. Their life had its ups and downs. They struggled through the Great Depression in the 1930's, renting out their house in Birmingham and traveling by car with their three children throughout the south as Bill taught marketing to car dealerships. They returned to Michigan; twice moving back to Fenton to care for Martha Collins Colwell and later Mabel Corrigan Phillips. Two of their children graduated from Fenton High School. When Bill went to work for Ford Motor Co. they moved to 90 Edison in the Boston Edison District in Detroit. This was the house built by Horace Rackham. When Mary Rackham died she willed the huge beautiful house to Nellie Scott. Bill later started a successful automotive distribution business, Adistra. Nellie was always the proper lady, but with a sly sense of humor. They kept the cottage on Crane's Point on Lake Fenton for many years, remodeling it into their full time house. Later they retired to Florida. They traveled extensively including a cruise on the final voyage of the Queen Mary. Bill and Nellie became Gramp and Nonie to fourteen grandchildren.

### Bay View Club of Fenton

The Bay View Club was started as a reading circle in 1897. Originally it was limited to 12 members and the ladies met every Thursday afternoon at 2:30. Their constitution stated that they organized "for the purpose of study and sociability" and meetings often included presentations and sketches of current and historical events. In June 1900, they had a picnic on Long Lake that became an annual event. July 1, 1909, their annual picnic was at the "handsome cottage of the president, Mrs. L.E. Becker." There was a 1 PM lunch, roaming the grounds, riding, and a meeting at 3 PM. At 5 PM, the gentlemen arrived. In 1913, they had expanded their membership. The President was Mrs. L.E. Becker, the Vice President was Mrs. C.A. Thompson, and the Secretary and Treasurer was Mrs. C.J. Phillips. The club visited the Detroit Museum of Art on December 6, 1921. In 1922, Mrs. C. J. Phillips was the president and she and Mrs. L.E. Becker were delegates to the State Federation of Women's Clubs. The original minutes of the meetings from 1987 to 1970 may be found at the Bennett Library on the Campus of the University of Michigan in Ann Arbor.


**Flu Pandemic**

From January 1918 to December 1920, a particularly deadly flu virus infected 500 million people across the world and resulted in the deaths of 50–100 million (3% – 5% of the world's population). Unlike most influenza outbreaks that disproportionately kill juvenile, elderly or already weakened patients, the 1918 pandemic predominantly killed previously healthy young adults. Although it has been speculated that this strain was particularly aggressive, more recent medical reports state that special circumstances (malnourishment, overcrowded medical camps and hospitals, poor hygiene) promoted a bacterial super–infection that killed most of the victims. Wartime censors minimized early reports of illness in Germany, Britain, France and the United States. However, papers in neutral Spain were free to report the epidemic's effects, creating a false impression that Spain was especially hard hit. This gave rise to the nickname "Spanish Flu."


**Long Lake/ Lake Fenton**

The lake north of Fenton currently called Lake Fenton was originally named Long Lake. In 1932, a petition was filed noting that there were 106 Long Lakes in the state of Michigan and the name should be changed to something more distinctive. Many long–time residents were bitter, but the name was changed to Lake Fenton. I've used the name Lake Fenton throughout for clarity.


**O.E. Williams School of Aviation**

In 1915 O.E. Williams came to Flint to repair an aeroplane owned by the Armstrong Company. Williams was impressed with the area and decided to relocate his flying school to Fenton. The village welcomed him enthusiastically, holding several town meetings to secure permanent quarters and funding. With the help of a workforce and a large class of students laboring day and night, Williams built a two–seater plane with dual controls for training. It had a 120 horsepower motor and was capable of 90 mph. It was taken out to the ice on Lake Fenton for its first flight. By spring, students were training on farmland owned by Tony Dauner. Their tuition was $250 each. The students were young and far from home and the people of Fenton held a number of social events on their behalf. An "Aviation Ball" was held at Cook's Opera House February 18, 1916. It was planned by the fifteen student pilots, and ladies were admitted for free. These pilots went on to fly for fairs and exhibitions. They even carried mail across the Detroit River to Windsor and Walkersville, Ontario. The Great War disrupted the future of William's Flying School as many of the exhibition fliers were called to active duty. The twelve original pilots were commemorated by the Fenton Chamber of Commerce on Memorial Day 1929 for giving their lives for the success of aviation.

# Bibliography

"A Time to Remember Fenton 1894 to Now" by Ruth Anne Silbar

A. J. Phillips and Sons Workmen's Time Book 1/26/1889– 5/4/1889

"American Victorian Costume in Early Photographs" by Priscilla Harris Dalrymple

"At Home" by Bill Bryson

Bay View Club Minutes 1897–1970 at the Bentley Historical Library at U of M

"Biography of an Endowment – The Horace H. Rackham and Mary A. Rackham Fund at the University of Michigan" by Marjorie Cahn Brazer

"Born Strangers" by Helen Topping Miller

"Burns Fuller Remembers: Fenton My Home Town" by Burns Fuller

"City of Promise" by Beverly Swerling

"Clara and Mr. Tiffany" by Susan Vreeland

"Decades of the 20th Century 1900s" published by Eldorado Ink

"Decades of the 20th Century 1910s" published by Eldorado Ink

Diary of Amelia Forte–1918 & 1930

Eighty Years of Growth, Personal Philosophies" by William C. Scott

"Fenton as He Knew It" Memories by Leo Weigant

Fenton High School yearbook "The Fentonian" 1904, 1908 & 1912

Fenton Independent Newspaper

- 1894 obituary of Judson B. Phillips
- 1904 "Class of '04"
- 7/1/1905–"June Weddings Phillips–Corrigan"
- 12/11/1913–"The A.J. Phillips Company Exchanges Plant for Detroit Property"
- 10/16/1919–"Passing of Colin Corrigan"
- 1926–"Charles Corrigan Prominent Citizen Dead after Prolonged Illness,
- 1926–"Judge Corrigan was Justice for 29 Years"
- 1926–"Charles Corrigan Prominent Citizen Dead after Prolonged Illness, Justice for past 29 years here"
- 1930–"Mrs. Allan Gunning Passed Away Sunday"
- 11/14/1943–obituary "Mrs. Clifford J. Phillips"
- 9/2/1965 – "Burns Fuller Remembers: Phillips Factory and Clan had much to do with Fenton"
- 8/18/1966–"When Steamboats Cruised Lake Fenton" by Ruth Anne Silbar
- 9/22/1966–" 'City of Flint' could carry 800 Passengers"
- 5/25/1967–"Fenton's Early Birds Are Remembered" by Ruth Ann Silbar
- 7/3/1969–"A.J. Phillips Gave Fenton Its Library Building"

- 8/8/1969–"Miniature Lamp Posts Recall Lake Fenton Hotels" by John Cox
- 11/19/1970–"Rare Photo of Latimer Hall Found" by John A Cox
- 3/11/1971–"A Time to Remember: Businesses and Industries of Fenton"
- 10/7/1971–"Ginsegagen–The Long Lake" by J. C. "Jace" Peck
- 11/25/1971–"Fenton High School–First 100 years Graduates of Early 1900s Still Alive"
- 11/9/1972–"How Fenton's Largest 19th Century Plant Grew" by Jan Rynearson
- 1/29/1976–"A Time to remember: The A. J. Phillips Public Library"
- 6/22/1978–"Old Directory describes lake life on Lake Fenton" by Jan Rynearson–Dean
- 11/16/1978–"From the Memoirs of Miss Alice Van Atta" as told to Jan Rynearson and the Dibbleville Questers
- 1/19/1983–"Down from the Attic"
- 1/19/83 – "Fenton area earns national historic rating" by Jan Rynearson–Dean
- 2/8/1984 "150th Celebration–Celebration recalls the Fenton that was..."
- 2/22/84 "Believe it, or not! Unique Fenton homes once drew Ripley's attention"
- 1/1/2000 "100 Years in Local History"
- "A Neighbor" Dr. Jefferson Gould
- "Everybody Knows Them, Phillips Started in Fenton in 1870"
- "Historical Society Hears Story of A. J. Phillips Co" by Basil Chappelle
- "Race to File Land Claim" by Bessie Gould

"Fenton Postcard History Series" by Donna and Kenneth Seger

"Fenton Public Schools Handbook 1904"

"Food in the United States, 1820s–1890" by Susan Williams

Glendale Daily Press 6/16/23–"To Celebrate Opening of Home for Dodge Brothers Cars Monday Night"

"History of Genesee County, Michigan Volume I & II" by Edwin O. Wood

"How to be a Victorian" by Ruth Goodman

"Junior Exhibition" program 1903

"Men, Wind and Courage A Pioneer Aviation Story of O. E. Williams and his Associates" by Nancy Lynn Mess

Michigan Military Academy booklet – 1898

"Oh! For the Life of a Country Girl: An Autobiography 1900–1984" by Edna H. Mitchell

Phillips Screen Goods Catalog "B"

"Quotations of Quality" by Sarah A. Crisman

"Ragtime" by Doctorow

"Reflections on a Bygone Era" by Alice Van Atta

Souvenir Program 125th Anniversary and Homecoming of Fenton, Michigan

"The American Family Home 1800–1960 by Clifford Edward Clark, Jr.

The Flint Journal
- 9/5/79 "A 91–year–old with 88 keys to a long life" by Kim Crawford
- 10/15/61–"Lake Fenton Once Had an Indian War" by Joyce S Cook

"The Great Influenza" by John M. Barry

The Fenton Courier 8/2/45–"Witnesses NY Tragedy Clifford J Phillips sees Bomber Crash"

"The Meaning of Names" by Karen Gettert Shoemaker

"The Rise of a Country Boy" by Terry Ferrel Allen

The Sunday News Magazine 5/19/74–"How Canfield's Citizens are Fighting to Save a Street"

"The Village Players at War 1942–1945" by Robert Harris

"This Victorian Life Modern Adventures in Nineteenth–Century Culture, Cooking, Fashion and Technology" by Sarah A. Chrisman

Tri–County News
- 1/17/83–"Historic Fenton Sites make National Register" by Bruce McLaughian
- 7/6/81–"Another Performance for Fenton's Opera House" by Cliff Peters

"True Ladies and Proper Gentlemen" by Sarah A. Chrisman

"Tyrone Revisited 1834–1976 A Bicentennial Salute" by Connie Riddell

"Victorian Secrets What a Corset Taught Me about the Past, the Present, and Myself" by Sarah A Chrisman

"What the Lady Wants: a Novel of Marshall Field" by Renee Rosen

"Webb's Freemason's Monitor" by Thomas Smith Webb

# About the Author

Marcina McKeon Foster is from Plymouth, Michigan and currently resides in Naples, Florida. She has a Bachelor of Science in English Language and Literature from Eastern Michigan University. As a young child she spent summers at her grandparents' cottage on Lake Fenton. The cottage was filled with many fascinating antiques and curiosities; two large hand cranked Victrolas with old WWI records, a wooden washstand with a fold down copper sink and shoe shine drawer, a pink flapper wedding dress and large skeleton key allegedly from the Tower of London. She was especially intrigued by the black and white pictures in a tooled leather photo album stored on a shelf in her grandmother's closet. There were pictures of little girls with huge bows in their hair, ladies in long dresses with bustles and huge hats and men in their stiff collars and formal suits sitting in antique cars. Although both her parents were from Fenton she knew little of the history of the Village or the role her ancestors played there, until she found a mysterious letter and set out to unravel its clues. Digging through family lore and memorabilia, visiting her parents' hometown, researching at historical libraries, she's taken a trip back to the turn of the last century to bring her family's story to life.

# Acknowledgments

So many people have been instrumental in helping me with this book. First and foremost I want to thank my sister Jean McKeon Martin who has collaborated with me for the last six years from the first trek into Fenton with camera and pencil to the final editing and last minute creative suggestions. She found time to do this while researching her own extensive genealogy project. Also, without the research and work of my grandfather William Colwell Scott and my uncle William Phillip Scott in the 1970's this book would not have been possible. They interviewed people and compiled a seven generation family tree and a notebook of ancestors' biographical information, pictures and interesting anecdotes. Much of their work was based on genealogy compiled by Walter Scott, past historian for the Mayflower Society in the 1940's.

This project was sparked by a letter written by Elizabeth (Bessie) Shields, my great grandfather's half–sister and in her own right she had done considerable research into the family's history.

Much of my research has been at the A. J. Phillips Historical Museum in Fenton, Michigan, and Connie Foley and Kim Wheeler have been extremely helpful locating information and photographs. Donna and Ken Seeger were most gracious in opening the Museum up to us and Doug Tabo gave us a tour of Oakwood Cemetery and explained the cemetery record keeping. In addition I'd like to acknowledge the research librarians at the Benson Ford Research Center in Dearborn, the Bentley 'Historical Library at the University of Michigan in Ann Arbor, and the Dunning–Hough Library in Plymouth who have all been very patient and helpful.

In the course of my research I found second cousins once removed, Richard Bennett, Dan Svenson and Jane Fortune in California who have provided invaluable information, photos and a 1918 diary for a branch of the family we knew little about. My cousin Sheree Posthumus and her husband John also owned many of the artifacts described in the book and generously shared pictures and information with me.

As I talked to friends about my project almost everyone had a connection or something to add to this project. The son of a good friend, Greg Wallace, and his daughter, Emily Wallace, happened to live in Glendale, California. They went to the Glendale Historical Society and researched my great great uncle Ray Corrigan, who had moved there after World War I.

I want to thank my niece Rachel Pearson for introducing me to my developmental editor, Terie Spencer, who stepped in when I hit a roadblock, reignited my passion for the project and continued to work with me to complete the manuscript.

I also want to thank my graphic designer, Theresa Fiorani at Canoe Circle Graphics, for the layout and design of the book and creating the cover design. She has taken the concept I could only imagine and made it reality, only better.

The artwork on the cover is an original acrylic painting "House on the Corner" by William Brody of Holly, Michigan. I am in awe of Mr. Brody's incredible art and was so fortunate that he had painted a picture of my great grandfather's house on Main Street in Fenton and generously allowed me to use it.

My friend Gigi Langer has been a font of information as she has written and published her own book, "50 Ways to Worry Less Now." She has guided me along the way from my first meeting with a writer's group, to providing information on publication, marketing and promotion. Ginna Jordan, MS in Historic Preservation at Eastern Michigan University, has helped me identify styles of architecture and date photos based on clothing and furnishings. Kathy Harenda has also patiently read the early versions and provided support.

Finally, I would like to thank my Beta Readers for their input; Jennifer Pittam from the UK for her suggestions regarding Clifford's visit to England, Harriet Lay at the Genesee County Historical Society, Rebecca Horvath, Joelle Brown, Joanne Pence and Julia Burmesch.

CPSIA information can be obtained
at www.ICGtesting.com
Printed in the USA
LVHW081318010820
661946LV00032B/534